This special
signed edition of

ODINS GIRL

is limited to 100 copies.

Kim Wilkins

ODIN'S GIRL

KIM
WILKINS

ODIN'S
GIRL

PS Australia

First Edition

ISBN
978-1-78636-208-7 (Signed Edition)
978-1-78636-209-4

2 4 6 8 10 9 7 5 3 1

Design and layout by Alligator Tree Graphics.

Printed in England by T. J. International.

PS Publishing Ltd / Grosvenor House /
1 New Road / Hornsea, HU18 1PG / England

editor@pspublishing.co.uk / www.pspublishing.co.uk

For my daughter Astrid:
Strength of the Aesir

CONTENTS

ODIN'S
GIRL

I

WILD
DREAMS
OF BLOOD

"I've never seen a bride with such sharp teeth"

—*Thrymsqvitha*

CHAPTER ONE

HARMONY

OMEWHERE, BENEATH THE SOUND OF flesh smashing into flesh, beneath the rattle of the cage, beneath the barking cheers, Sara Jones could hear music. A happy twanging song, out of sync with the chaotic rhythm of sweat and phlegm and blood. She tuned in to it, trying to follow its melody. Country music, perhaps? A woman singing. It brought a touch of the carnivalesque to the grim cavernous arena. She became more aware of the colours in the room: the bright yellow of the lights, the brilliant blue of a fighter's headband, the deep red floor.

"He's in the fence! He's in the fence!" The announcer's harsh voice slapped around the auditorium. The crowd throbbed; the heat in the room noticeably increased. The smell of men and dirt and rubber under hot lights. Sara breathed it in, her nostrils twitching. What she really wanted to smell was the iron tang of blood, but she was too far away from the action for that. The Tall Man was going down: six foot six of densely coiled muscle, but the doughy man a foot shorter with the blue headband—Blue, she called him—was pummelling him into the side of the cage. The Tall Man's feet began to slip out from under him. He had been the favourite, the one everybody had come to see win. Elimination style. An upset. Blue pounded Tall Man. Blood poured from Blue's nose, as though the effort it took to defeat his opponent had burst something in his head. Down went Tall Man. Down.

All the way down.

The hooter sounded, harsh and final.

"And there's your winner! There's your winner!" The announcer's voice was rapturous, a preacher in full ecstasy. Blue collapsed to his knees, threw his arms around his opponent to help him up. They hugged, slapping each other's bare backs. Then Blue raised his arms triumphant. A shapely woman—possibly the only other female body besides Sara's in the auditorium—emerged with a sash and a trophy. The season was over. The winner had been crowned.

The season was over. No more sneaking out with flimsy excuses on her tongue. The arena would close down for three months, the fighters would stay home and let their wounds heal. And Sara would go back to her wild dreams. She felt an icy itch in her stomach.

She sat in her plastic seat while the arena emptied. The music played on: harmonicas and plaintive singing. It was long past time to go home. Would Dillon be worried? Her mobile phone was still switched off in her handbag. She'd tell him the flight was late. It wasn't in Dillon's nature to investigate, and she went away for work a lot. Luckily for her, the arena was in an industrial estate just off the

6

highway on the long drive from the airport. If she timed her trips interstate just right, she nearly always managed to see a fight on her way out or back.

Two janitors were making their way through the arena, row by row, picking up rubbish and cigarette butts. A third slopped sharp-smelling disinfectant across the floor of the cage. Sara looked around. Everyone else was gone.

Outside, the air was soft and laced with the smell of salt coming off the sea. This side of town, near the airport and the seaport, was flat and laid out with shipping yards, storage barns, and pumping stations. A plane thundered overhead. She watched its lights blinking code back to air traffic control. She'd never seen a plane fly that low over Harmony Square and she'd lived there since she was a child. It was the other side of town, other side of the highway. Manicured lawns and shopping strips. Somebody rich would whine if a plane dared to rattle their windows.

Sara's little turquoise Suzuki was the last car left in the dirt lot. While she warmed up the engine, she switched on her mobile phone. Three text messages from Dillon. *Where are you? You back safe? Let me know when you land.*

She quickly replied. *On my way.* And pulled out onto the road.

She hit the highway eight minutes later, listening to Norwegian death metal so loud it made the speakers jump. It was the only music that massaged the prickling part of her that longed for violence. Dillon had caught her listening to it once and she'd pretended it was the radio, that she'd somehow ended up on the wrong station. She was more careful now, hiding the CD deep in the back of the glove box. Not that they often took her car anywhere. Dillon was proud of his new Audi and, while a twenty-first century man in most respects, he still held onto the shred of a conviction that women weren't good drivers.

The road was eleven-p.m. quiet. She passed an occasional truck going the other way. One set of tail lights in front of her. The silent pine forest either side of the road. She drummed on her steering wheel.

Then the tail lights in front of her swerved, and she instinctively stabbed at her own brakes. The car ahead left the road at high speed, clipping the ditch and flipping, rolling into the trees. Sara had already pulled onto the shoulder before it came to rest. She cut her engine and the clattering music abruptly stopped. Silence. Her ticking engine.

She grabbed the torch from her glove box, opened the door and climbed out. The air was cold on her skin. She ran ahead the fifty metres to the other car, heart pounding. The smell of petrol. His tank had been punctured. The engine was still whirring, hot.

"Shit," she said, shining her torch inside. The car was upside down. Hanging from his seatbelt, unconscious, was Tall Man from the cage fight.

Six foot six of densely coiled muscle.

Sara looked around helplessly. No other cars. She could call emergency, but they would take too long to get out here.

Sara felt the tingle in her muscles, a foretaste of the thing she wasn't supposed to do, a guilty frisson at finally letting the dog off the leash. This was life or death, right? And nobody was watching. She rounded the front of the car and grasped its bumper bar in both hands, took a breath, and lightly flipped the car back onto its tyres. It landed with a crunch, rocked once on its suspension, then was still.

Sara wrenched open the crumpled door and half-climbed in. Reached over and unclicked his seatbelt. The smell of blood made her nose twitch.

"Wassss?" he said.

"Sh. I'm going to get you out."

She tugged and he was over her shoulder. She backed out of the car with the man worn around her shoulders like a burly scarf. A rough breeze tousled the long grass on the side of the road as she walked away from the wreck, which would almost certainly ignite. Her skin stood out in goosebumps. In the stony ditch beside her own car, she tucked him safely on his side. Her heart flickered and fluttered with the blue-white thrill of it. "You're safe," she said, brushing his bloody hair from his eyes with her thumb. "But I have to go."

Her feet crunched on the gravel. She started her car. A truck roared past but she didn't hear it over her music. She saw it touch its brakes as the driver spotted the crumpled car on the side of the road. Good: somebody else would call the accident in. She accelerated away, passed the truck. A bloom of orange light in her rear-view mirror told her that Tall Man's car had caught fire. Sara didn't look back.

In the harsh bright light of the roadhouse washroom, she studied herself in the mirror. A bloody smear across her pale cheek. A torn seam between shoulder and collar on her dress. Mud on her elbows. She cleaned and tidied herself. What she couldn't see in the mirror was the underneath. The hard-pumping blood, the sharp sparkling adrenalin, and the guilty fear. If anyone found out, her whole world would crumble.

"That took a long time," Dillon said, as she pushed open the door to their townhouse.

"Sorry," she said.

"Here, let me get that." He took her suitcase. "You look exhausted."

He headed upstairs while she dropped her keys on the kitchen bench and quickly glanced through the mail. Bank statements, prize homes, charities.

"There was an accident on the highway," she called, by way of an explanation for her late arrival. It wasn't a lie.

"It's okay," he called. "I've been catching up on my ironing."

She could see that. The ironing board, the smell of starch. He always started ironing right before she was due home. Her job was to notice he was doing it badly and offer to take over. She was very good at ironing shirts.

"Tell you what," she said as he emerged from the staircase, "you make me something to eat and I'll finish these shirts for you."

"Would you?"

"Of course."

He smiled, and his eyes crinkled at the corners. Five years on, and that smile could still make her heart flip over as it had that first time she'd seen him, sun in his dark hair, on the grass at Harmony U.

"Is a toasted sandwich okay?" he asked.

"As long as it's one of your pizza specials," she said.

"Got it."

He was in the kitchen, adding tomato paste, cheese, and pineapple to a sandwich for her. He was whistling and she thought, *he sounds merry.*

And she picked up the next shirt in the pile to give it a shake. Something fell out. Landed right between her feet. The lamplight caught its sparkle.

She bent to pick it up. It was cold between her fingers. When she stood, he was there, smiling at her.

"You'll marry me, won't you, Sara?"

Sara had crushed her grandmother's index finger at three months of age. Turned the bone to sawdust. By ten months she had broken six cots and her mother gave up and let her share the double bed. Nobody was allowed to give her wooden toys. Wood, for some reason, aroused more acutely the desire to break and crush. She fared better with stuffed teddies, which she loved to cuddle and stroke. As though their lack of resistance to the world made them safe from her unquenchable desire to smash everything to pulp.

By her third birthday, she was starting to learn self-control. As strong as she was, she still hadn't worked out the buttons on the remote control. The threat of missing *Playschool* could make her behave. Then Disney princesses taught her meek beauty. She couldn't plough her shoulder into the wall as fast in pink plastic high-heels.

But she was always aware of the dark thing inside her. It thrilled her and it frightened her, and she quickly learned to be ashamed of it; though the shame didn't make it go away. Behind the long back yard was an empty block, and she spent furtive hours every afternoon breaking branches, turning over rocks, chucking broken bricks into the iron fence. School was hard: so many other children to get along with. They had to move town four times, change schools, start over. Broken monkey bars; water bubblers wrenched off their weldings; a whiteboard eraser thrown so hard at the wall that it made a hole through the plasterboard and sailed through to the other side.

By sixth grade she was fatigued from being the new kid. She learned to be gentle. She learned to pull the rage out of her hands and arms, compress it into a white-hot ball behind her ribs. She sometimes broke a desk or a chair by accident, and gained a reputation among her teachers for being clumsy. Of course. A girl her size had to be clumsy.

That was it. She came to heel.

Only that wasn't it. There was one other incident, wasn't there? She just didn't like to remember it. High school, bitchy teenage girls, a Queen Bee. Sara always kept her eyes down, but she nudged six foot, with red-gold hair and generous curves. She couldn't stay invisible. The rage bubbled over. It seemed so long ago, now, since she had felt that power move up through her veins and sinews . . .

Sara had seen Queen Bee just two weeks ago, across the road in the distance: she was still in the wheelchair. The clumsy-fingered churn of guilt had started all over again. Nobody had been around to witness that fight. The injuries weren't consistent with a schoolyard smackdown, so nobody believed Queen Bee and, of course, Sara denied everything.

Sara was used to denying everything.

"It's just so old-fashioned, Mum." Sara shook the newspaper and placed it on the wrought-iron seat next to her. The oily smell of the newsprint mingled unpleasantly with the smell of tea brewing, fresh cane mulch, cut grass. Her mother's garden in Harmony Square was immaculately kept and a little old-fashioned: and so was Mother.

"I've been dreaming about the day I could put a wedding announcement in the *Harmony Times*, Sara. Don't deny me the pleasure."

"I've been getting congratulatory calls from old school friends . . . not that they were ever friends," Sara said.

"School was ten years ago. Everyone's forgiven you for being odd. They can be your friends now. A big wedding can be such a happy occasion."

Sara sat back, smiling bemusedly at Mother. "I don't want a big wedding, and I definitely don't want to invite people I used to go to school with."

Mother was perpetually prompting Sara to contact old friends or make new ones. But Sara found keeping friends difficult. Sooner or later, they sensed she wasn't telling them the whole truth about herself.

"It's silly to have your mother as your bridesmaid."

"Maid of honour. Please, Mum, don't make a huge fuss. Short engagement, just family, in the gardens next to the birch wood. Really, that's all I want."

Mother plucked a cupcake off the plate and offered one to Sara, who refused it with a raised hand.

"I can't. Wedding dress fittings coming up."

"You're beautiful exactly as you are," Mother said, but the words sounded hollow. Exactly what she was had always been a problem for both of them.

Long ago, Mother had taken to calling her unnatural strength 'your thing', a euphemism on equal footing with 'number twos' and 'monthly visitor'. When they'd moved to Harmony Square, she'd resolutely refused to talk about it anymore. "Don't let *your thing* ruin it," she'd said. "And don't mention it to anyone. We have a new beginning here."

Sara knew what Harmony Square meant to Mother. Years as a single parent, struggling on a combination of welfare and low-paid part-time jobs. Finally falling in love with her Chairman-of-the-Board boss when Sara was nine. Pete lived on the good side of the highway and invited them to share that life with him. Everything changed for them. Mother didn't have to struggle anymore. It seemed to Sara that her mother had shed twenty years off her face in the first two months in Harmony Square. Her determination never to go back to the bad side of the highway made Mother steely in a way that could be mistaken for coldness, conservative as an old lady despite her relative youth.

"I've been thinking . . . " Sara started, but stopped herself.

"Go on."

She inhaled. "I'm getting married. And usually at a wedding, there's a father of the bride. To give me away."

The tightness around Mother's mouth confirmed Sara's first instinct. Don't bring it up. Never bring it up.

But this time, instead of screeching at Sara, Mother put her teacup on the patio table with shaking hands, smoothed her hair, and said, "You have no father."

"Yes, I do. Somewhere in the world. I know you don't want me to contact him, but—"

"You have no father," Mother said, more forcefully. "I always intended to tell you the truth, and I need you to get out of your head any notion that there might be a loving reunion in time for your wedding. Get it out of your head."

"Mum, I—"

"When I say you have no father, I don't mean I hate him and want to forget he exists, Sara. There was nobody. Nobody. I was pregnant at seventeen and everybody assumed I was the kind of girl who got knocked up at a party. I wasn't. I didn't. I was a virgin on the day you were born."

Sara felt the tick of her heart in her throat. Mother was flushed.

"You have no father," Mother said again. "I promise you."

Her mind whirled. "Then how—"

"Don't," Mother said, a hand raised in warning. "I won't say another word. Now, more tea?"

The dreams are always in the same location. She stands outside the doors of a wooden hall, its boards stained black from years of damp and smoke. The hall faces north: the chill drifts down towards her, prickling her nostrils. A sunless place; churning clouds eat the sky. They reflect in the dark river that runs through the valley, carving its course into stony ground between thousands upon thousands of spears and swords, sprouting like saplings all around her.

In the river there are bodies. Wolves on the banks pull drowned men onto land to eat them. The smell of blood is everywhere, and Sara's dream body tingles with excitement. Bare-handed and alone, she waits. Then they come. One at a time, wading through the heavy currents of the river.

Murderers, betrayers, oath-breakers. Grim men with hulking bodies and darkly glittering eyes. Some nights there are dozens, some nights there are only a few, but she knows what she must do with them, even though she doesn't know why she must do it.

The revolution inside her body is as thrilling as it is terrifying. As they approach her, raise their arms to push her out of their way and get inside the hall, she seizes them, throws them to the ground, stamps on their heads, kneels on their bellies and pummels them senseless, tears at their faces, dislocates their joints, and snaps their sinews. Something beyond rage is in control of her. It smells like animal and it pours down through her limbs with the speed of a river, the heat of lava, and the weight of iron. She shrieks and the sound echoes through the valley. It is the deathly baying of a trapped beast.

Soft, bell-like music. Sara opened her eyes and the world—the real world—rushed back in. The pale blue colours of the bedroom she shared with Dillon, the dewy sunlight through the gauzy curtains, the soft comfort of her pillows. Quiet. Order. The dream vanished with a snap, leaving only the echo of the wild chaos tingling along her veins. She took a breath. She'd had the dream hundreds of times before, but never grew used to it. Under the covers, she flexed her arm, felt the searing preternatural strength buried under her white skin. No outward sign of it gave her secret away, no muscle. If anything, she always felt as though she looked doughy; not sleek enough.

"Coffee, Sara?"

"Yes, please." Every morning when the alarm went off, Dillon got up and made coffee and toast for them both, and brought it back to bed. She hadn't made herself breakfast in two years.

He kissed her cheek. "Back in a few minutes."

She watched as he threw back the covers, the solid plane of his tanned back disappearing into black cotton boxer shorts. She smiled. Soon she would call him her husband, and the thought gave her a warm glow. Husband. Wife. New words unlocked into her vocabulary.

He looked back at her, saw her smiling. "You look happy."

"I am."

"So am I. I'm glad you're in my life."

But it had been different when he first met her. Dillon had been deeply and desperately in love—the unrequited kind—with Sara's classmate, Emily Pascoe. Emily was everything Sara wasn't: petite and slim, with glossy dark hair, and poreless olive skin. They'd all been in their third year at Harmony U together. Dillon had pressed Sara into service to help him woo Emily. Sara did everything he asked because she was deeply and desperately in love—the unrequited kind—with Dillon. Finally, Emily broke his heart and moved to the other side of the country. Dillon turned to Sara. Their close friendship grew into love.

Sara had seen Dillon's passionate side: the stormy seas that Emily had aroused in his heart. But she hadn't seen it since. She presumed she wasn't the kind of woman who aroused stormy seas. They laughed a lot together, they liked the same movies, they got along. He had probably never got over Emily. But she didn't ask. She was busy protecting him from her own uncomfortable truth.

17

Harmony Square was bordered on the north and the west with woodland. Mostly silver birches, which meant that even in the densest sections, the silver-grey trunks and yellow-green leaves held onto the sunlight. A path led through it for six kilometres, and it was a popular place to walk dogs or go jogging. Dawn and dusk were busy and safe, but Sara had timed her run badly. First, she'd finished work late. Then, she'd been stuck behind a council truck on the main street and missed every green light. Finally, she'd returned to the house to change her socks—her middle toe kept slipping uncomfortably through a hole in the seam—and the way Dillon sorted laundry meant it had taken just a fraction too long. The sun was down before she was two kilometres in, and it was only at night that the shadows in the wood gathered thickly enough that she might lose her footing.

She hesitated, thought about turning back. But wedding dress fittings were on her mind. Sara knew she couldn't fight her generous breasts and her round hips, but she was determined at least to find the lean edge on her arms so she could wear something sleeveless in the spring sunshine.

So she kept running. She passed an elderly man with an elderly dog. He said good evening as he shuffled past. Then nobody else. Her huffing breath. Her footfalls. The occasional late-to-bed bird. Leaves falling with a soft clatter deep in the wood. Distant traffic. A soft breeze.

One foot in front of the other. She was coming to the crook in the path. In one direction, she could run an extra kilometre and come out at the river. But if she hairpinned back she'd be on her way home again: the run half over.

She rounded the crook and began the home stretch. The darkness now was comprehensive. If there was dog shit on the path, she would step on it. If there were noises she couldn't make sense of in the woods, she simply had to ignore them. She was gripped by a powerful desire to be home at her empty house—Dillon was away for two nights on business—to have a warm shower and eat something.

Because there were footfalls. Not on the path, but in the wood. Heavy footfalls. Not lumbering. Fast and purposeful.

Sara stepped up the pace. Her heart pounded. The thing making that noise was keeping pace with her, but amongst the trees. How it found its way around low-hanging branches and fallen logs in the dark was a mystery. But it was more than the footfalls that unnerved her, because Sara was strong; stronger than anyone: no masked man could knock her off her feet. It was something else, a tingling of primitive fear, a heightened sense of awareness that sent stony dread rocketing through all her limbs. A judgement was coming, something mighty and ancient. She sensed it with something beyond sight and sound. She smelled it with her gut.

At last she burst from the wood. Across the green she could see her back fence, the light left on in the upstairs bedroom. She tore across the open space, and the hulking shadow was behind-beside her. She didn't look, she kept her head down.

Through the gate, slamming it in his face. For it was a man, a huge man with an equally huge beard. Fumbled her keys. Got in the house. Locked the door. Reached for the phone.

The line was dead. She could see him through the kitchen window, scaling the six-foot back fence. Meaty hands, long muscular legs. A man-monster. If she ran out the front door, he would intercept her there. No, she would have to stay and fight. As his feet landed in her garden, the electricity fizzed. The kitchen lights browned down, then winked off: the strange unexpected silence when fridges stop humming.

Sara caught her breath. He knocked loudly on the sliding door.

Sara came out of hiding, faced him through the glass. He was in shadows, a felt hat pulled down low, a black shadow over his left eye.

"Who are you?" she demanded.

"Odin Allfather."

A slithering snake of cold discomfort and familiar longing stirred inside her.

"Go away," she said. "Go away or I'll come out there and tear your head off."

To her surprise, he smiled broadly. Not cruelly. "That's my girl."

She frowned.

"Let me in," he said. "I'm your father."

CHAPTER TWO
THROUGH
A PINHOLE

S ARA DIDN'T DOUBT HE WAS TELLING THE
truth. Here, inside, by the light of the kerosene
lamp, the resemblance between them was evident.
He'd taken off his hat and now she could see the same red-gold hair,
the same straight-tipped nose and generous mouth. She looked closely
at his remaining eye—the other was covered with a patch—and it was
the same icy blue as her eyes. Her fatherless state had meant she paid
close attention to the similarities between Mother and herself. Sometimes she had imagined them, needing to feel she belonged, that she
had provenance.

Here was where she came from. Without doubt.

Sara became aware of all the tiny sounds normally hidden by electricity. The thrum of her blood pressure, the tick of the clock in the

upstairs hallway, the distant traffic on the ring road that led to the City. Her skin prickled lightly.

"Why did the lights go out?" she asked him, after they had been silent, studying each other, for a long time.

"Magic."

"I see."

"I'm covered in it. It's quite a journey to get here. Don't worry. It will fade soon, and your electricity will work just fine."

"So . . . to get here from where?"

"Asgard."

"I see," she said again. Perhaps if she had been any other woman, with any other personal history, she would have thought him mad. But she had lived her whole life with supernatural strength. His explanation made the most sense of any she had conjured over the years. "And why come now?"

"You're getting married."

"You saw the announcement?" She felt as confused as that time she had fallen off the high fence outside her Mother's house, knocking herself out for a half-second. Reality swam a little, then coalesced again.

"Yes. No. It's complicated. News comes to me of you. I gather it in strange ways."

"Magic?"

He bowed his head in a nod. "It's easier to call it magic than to explain. All of you here in Midgard live in ignorance, as though you are looking at existence through a pinhole."

A tickle of promise, of feeling she belonged to something vast and powerful. She tried to form words, but couldn't, so decided to stick with the basic questions. "So you came to give me away? At my wedding?"

He looked around the kitchen, eye blinking slowly. Then his gaze rested on her once more. "You're too thin."

She stifled a laugh. "You're the first person to say that to me. Ever."

"Why do you live like this? I gave you divine strength. Why have you not conquered this place?"

She swallowed hard. "Harmony Square? It didn't require conquering."

"Why have you not been all you could be? Why have you not used your strength?"

Because I was ashamed of it. But she didn't tell him that. "I couldn't use it. How would I use it? Knocking down houses for a living?" Even as she said it, the thrill of the idea shimmered across her skin. The fantasy of tearing Mother's faux-Victorian mansion down with her hands, crushing it to perfumed dust.

He shifted in his chair, shoulder flexed forward, agitated. "When I created you, I had you thrown into the future. Into a time when women were allowed to rule. Why haven't you ruled?"

Sara blinked back at him. Her heart felt compressed, icy. "What do you mean by 'creating' me?"

"I sowed my seed in a young human woman. I could tell with my hands on her belly that it was you: Aesir strength, mortal heart. I didn't want you to be born in Norway in 987. I wanted you to be somewhere you could make use of your strength, so I cast you 1000 years into the future."

"How?"

The corners of his mouth turned up under his shaggy beard.

"Oh. Magic."

"I'm not here to celebrate your wedding, Daughter. This Dillon Kincaid, he is not a fit husband for you."

She knew that she should have felt defensive, but instead she just felt frightened. "Dillon's very sweet. He makes me coffee every morning. We understand each other. He's perfect for me."

"Is he? Is he now?" Odin stroked his beard thoughtfully. "Then he will have to prove himself to me."

Sara bristled. "He doesn't have to prove anything to you."

Odin stood, thrust out his hand with three fingers raised. "Three tests," he said. "Mind, heart, and body."

"This is ridiculous," Sara replied, panic lighting a fire along her veins. "You can't come here after twenty-four years and—"

"A thousand years!" he roared. "A thousand years, Daughter, and this is what I'm greeted with? You hiding your strength, ironing for him, not eating so you can fit into a frilly dress? Perhaps Dillon Kincaid is worth it, but that is for me to judge."

"And if he's not? Are you going to forbid me from marrying him? You said you sent me to a more enlightened time. Fathers can't decide who their daughters marry in *my* world."

He glared at her a moment, then softened. "I'm not going to forbid you. I only want to see his worth with my own eye." He pointed to his good eye theatrically, then turned his pointing finger around. "I want you to see with your eyes."

He rose, towering over her, and put a huge hand on her shoulder. Gently, infinitely gently. "My daughter. I mean you no harm."

"Then leave me be and let me live my life." Deep down hoping, hoping he would do the opposite.

"No," he said. "You will know when the tests have started."

"Don't hurt him."

"Let things fall the way they will fall."

The lights flickered and then burned into life. Sara blinked against the sudden brightness. Odin had already turned and was stalking away, through the tiny courtyard and through the gate. Sara put her head on the kitchen table. She had never been good at thinking. Not that she was stupid: far from it. It was just that thinking—deeply thinking, connecting thoughts with feelings and understanding herself—made her so tired. She had never felt more weary than she felt now, in the wake of her father's visit.

Her father.

Sara realised she was weeping.

A week passed. Two. Sara wondered whether Dillon had already passed all his tests. He had a good mind, a good heart, and he was strong in his own way. She didn't mention Odin to anyone. Not to Dillon, who didn't know her secret strength. Not to Mother, who didn't want to know about her secret strength. Not to any of her friends at work. The wild dreams still came regularly, but now she understood what they meant. It was as though meeting her father had awakened her to the deep, lost mysteries of her own blood. The building was Odin's: Valhalla, the hall where the glorious dead could celebrate eternally. She was stopping the inglorious dead from entering.

But she never got inside it either, and the idea made its way under her skin and itched like an ant bite. *What if I never get inside?* She could barely articulate why it was so important to her. Her life here—in Midgard, as Odin had called it—promised her all she needed: a good home, companionship, quiet days and weeks and years. But over there—Asgard—was the rough, thrilling mystery that had called to her in her muscles since she was born.

She tried to become lucid during the dreams, to wrench open the door and go in and see the glittering firelight, hear the clatter of music, and feel the warmth of the hearth and the company. If she could glimpse the inside of that mystery, just once, then she would return to her life in Midgard and be quiet and still as she'd ever intended. But every time she put her hand on the door, she would awake, at home in Harmony Square, Dillon breathing softly and evenly next to her.

She drove out to collect Dillon late one night from work, at a building site just outside the Square. He'd designed the internal architecture of a warehouse rebuild, turning it into a retail showroom, and he'd been working long hours after electrical problems had stalled the refit.

The warehouse stood in a garden of mud and discarded building supplies. The blue-white streetlight flickered as the wind stirred the branches lining the street. Sara picked her way across to the front door, which was open. "Hello?" she called out. Her voice echoed in the big empty space.

"Sara. Up here."

She looked up to the first floor landing, to see Dillon with his hard hat on and a rolled-up architectural plan under his arm.

"Come on up," he called. "I want to show you what we've been doing."

She closed the door behind her with an echoing thump. The interior was dimly illuminated by gas lamps. "Still no electricity?" she asked, clattering up the iron stairs.

"We've had to redesign where the wiring goes. We're behind but catching up." He grasped her hand at the top of the stairs, and pulled her across to the next staircase. "The best view is from up the top."

They reached the top floor landing and stood in the semi-dark looking down.

"You have to imagine it brightly lit, and full of shiny new things. Designer furniture. Or electrical goods."

Sara squinted as though it could help her picture plasma screens and leather couches arranged artfully on the wooden walls and floorboards.

"I'm so proud of it."

She turned to him, smiling. This was his first project since his promotion. "You should be." She reached her hand up to brush his hair away from his temple and, as she did so, her engagement ring flew off.

Flew. It didn't fall. It wasn't even loose. It flew, as though it had grown wings from the back of its solitary diamond, and then plummeted in a perfect arc—down and down—towards the ground floor.

Both of them tensed, waiting for the crack as it hit the ground. Nothing.

Dillon turned and headed for the stairs. Sara hurried after him.

"Where is it?" Dillon said, scanning the floor. The gas lamps created confusing shadows.

Sara's heart sped a little. "Do you have a torch?"

Dillon unclipped the torch from his belt and began to shine it around. Together they scanned every inch of the floor with the torchbeam.

"That cost me a month's salary," he grumbled. He looked up at her. "You've lost too much weight if your ring can slide off that easily. You'll need to get it resized."

Sara said nothing. Then a gleam caught her eye. "There!" she said.

Dillon aimed the torchbeam, then crouched on the floor, shining it directly into a knothole in the floorboard, about the size of a coin. "For Christ's sake. What kind of bad luck is that?"

Bad luck. Of course he would think it was bad luck. He didn't believe in magic.

"It's under the floorboards?"

Dillon sat back on his haunches. "Underneath here is the wiring and the under-floor heating. There's a crawl space, about this high." He held his hands two feet apart. "And your engagement ring has somehow found the only way through."

"Can we pull up the floorboards?"

He shook his head. "Not without costing the contractor more money. No, I'll go through the basement entrance then into the utility hatch. I've got a clear idea in my head of the floor plan, so I should be able to find it."

Now Sara understood. This was Odin's test of the mind for Dillon. Relief undid the knots in her stomach. She had never met anybody smarter than Dillon. He remembered credit card numbers and international time zones and postcodes. He could look at a route once on a map and find his way without a second glance. She reached out and touched his hair softly. "What do you want me to do?"

"Just wait up here." He lifted her hand and kissed it. "Watch me through the knothole if you like."

So she sat back on the smooth floorboards with her legs out and her palms propping her up. Was Odin nearby? Could she call out to him or speak to him? She brimmed with questions for him. But maybe it was best if she didn't ask them, in case it pitched her into lifelong yearning. She was Mother's daughter as much as Odin's; she belonged to this world as much as his. If not more.

Dillon's voice, muffled by floorboards. "I'm in."

She turned over, called through the knothole. "It's over this way."

"I know that. It's just . . . this is a bit trickier than I thought."

A flash of heat to her heart. "It's not dangerous, is it?"

"No, just tricky. It's like a maze under here. But I designed the maze, so if I can just remember where the junctions are and take it slow, I should be fine."

"Take good care." She tensed, waiting to hear his voice again. Instead she could hear bumping and slithering as he crawled through the utility space. A light buzzing feeling just under her skin. For some reason, her body was switching to alert.

Smoke. She could smell smoke.

Every sense lit up with cold electricity. "Dillon?" she called. "Dillon, I can smell smoke!"

She leaped to her feet, eyes darting madly. A thin curl of smoke emerged from between the floorboards about ten feet away, creeping closer to Dillon. She threw herself on the floor and hammered on the boards.

"Dillon!"

"Jesus Christ!" The bumping and slithering became frantic as he tried unsuccessfully to retrace the maze, backwards. Sara fumbled for her mobile phone to call emergency, but she knew she couldn't wait for a fire engine. She had to get Dillon out herself. The heat was travelling along the boards. It was under her hands, sizzling. She dropped her phone.

Sara stood, brought down her heel with heavy intent on the floor.

29

A board cracked. She got her hands underneath it and peeled it up, as easily as another woman might peel a banana. Then she pulled another up, and another. Smoke poured out but she could see no flame.

She put her hand through the hole, coughing, frantic. "Here, Dillon! Over here!"

Calling his name was like a spell. The smoke evaporated, sucked back into the air through hidden folds. She breathed. His hand grasped her wrist. She had to remind herself not to pull him. He clambered up through the hole in the floor with wild eyes. His shoes were gone.

He stared at her. "What just happened? Where's the fire?"

"I don't know. I . . . It just . . . disappeared."

His face screwed up. "How did you . . . ?" His eyes went to the hole she had torn in the floor.

"They must have been loose."

"Fucking electricians," he spat. "I could have died."

She reached into the utility space, withdrew her ring. "At least we found this." She slid it back onto her finger, her blood moving more slowly now.

He sat on the floor heavily, his head on his knees. "I could have died," he said again, under his breath.

"We should get out of here. We should call the fire brigade, just in case."

But he didn't move and she put her arms around him and clung to him, fighting tears. Dillon had failed the first test.

"My beautiful daughter. You take my breath away."

Sara spun in a slow circle. The bridal boutique was wall-to-wall with mirrors, and she saw her own statuesque body reflected infinitely around her. Smooth white skin, round shoulders, pale red hair. She was formed for midnight blue or dark crimson, but Mother wanted her in pale pink. Sara fought the conviction that she looked like a freshly picked scab. "Really? This colour, Mum?"

"It's so feminine. And you know I really don't like brides wearing white when they've been living with their fiancés for so long." Mother's mouth turned down in a ghost of disapproval, soon forgotten. "You always looked lovely in pink when you were little. The soft tones suit your skin."

Sara turned and viewed herself from all angles, craning her neck. It was a pretty colour, and Mother was often right about these things. What would Sara know about how to be a normal woman? She stooped to kiss Mother on the top of the head. "If you like this one the best . . ."

"It's your special day."

"It's special for you, too." Sara turned to the sales assistant. "This one."

The sales assistant ran about looking for pins and tape measures. Mother closed her eyes and bowed her head onto her hands.

"You okay, Mum?"

Mother looked up. "I feel old today, Sara."

"You're not old." Sara smiled. "You're still hot."

Mother tried to hide her own grin. "Well. Thank you."

"I bet Pete can't believe his luck." Pete was in his mid-sixties.

Mother pushed a stray hair off her own cheek. "Pete is a wonderful husband. And I know your Dillon will be just as wonderful." Mother's

31

eyes grew sharp, detecting something in Sara's expression. "What? What's wrong?"

Sara shrugged. "He's been a little distant the last week or so."

"You've been away interstate again. I don't know if it's a good idea for you to travel so much. He probably feels neglected."

"No. He's not that old-fashioned." She was almost certain she was right. Her contract at work was due to expire just before the wedding, and he'd encouraged her not to rush to find another one. "I think work is on his mind." The incident at the warehouse last month had not been kind to them. Dillon had to spend many hours back at the site, making the electricians go over the wiring repeatedly, organising floor repairs, calling in the engineers again for structure and safety tests. The finish date had been pushed back, and now the star employee was losing his company money. It made him grumpy, listless. He was a man who liked to get things right. Sara also suspected he was pondering how the events of the evening had happened at all, but she never raised it with him. Life had taught her to keep her head down and not engage with the mystery. People mostly saw what they had always seen.

Mother dropped her voice. "You haven't mentioned your questions about your father to him, have you?"

Sara was surprised to hear Mother raise the issue. "No. Of course not."

"Good. Because it's best forgotten."

Sara spread her hands. "It's forgotten then."

Mother smoothed her hair and looked around. "I wonder where that sales girl is?"

———

Sara hoped her father would come again. She wanted to tell him that she didn't care for his tests, that she was going to marry Dillon even if he failed every single one. But also, she simply wanted to see him again. She craved the weight of his arcane presence.

Then finally he returned. Dillon was working late at the warehouse and she was home alone eating a microwaved diet dinner and flicking through bridal sites on the internet. The lamp on her desk fizzed and the light went out. The computer screen went black. When the booming knock on the door came, she knew it was him. She rose with apprehension and longing in her heart.

"Father," she said.

"Daughter." He nodded, pulled off his hat. "I have been waiting for a chance to speak with you."

"Come in," she said, standing aside, and shutting the door after him.

He stopped at the computer desk, his hand on the back of the chair.

"Will you sit down?" she asked. She had no idea of the correct etiquette in this situation. "I'll get a candle."

"No, I won't sit down. And you don't need a candle. Your electricity will come on again soon enough. I have something important to say."

"Well, I do too," she said, gathering her courage.

He continued as if he hadn't heard her. "Dillon Kincaid failed the first test and—"

"He would have been fine if you hadn't started a fire," she replied sharply. "He found the ring."

"What is a mind if it cannot hold strong under pressure?"

"He was afraid of burning to death." She was swallowing over her heartbeat. "It would make any man confused."

"I don't want you to marry 'any man'. Remember who you are."

A strong sense of disappointment gripped her. She had hoped, on seeing him again, to find a connection with him. But he seemed only interested in criticising her. The disappointment caught her off-guard and she snapped. "I have only known who I am a few weeks. You have never been in my life. You can't come into it now and tell me what to do."

"I won't tell you what to do, but I can tell you what I think of your choices."

"I don't care what you think."

He threw up his hands in exasperation. "From what I see, you care what everyone else thinks."

Sara fell silent. Odin indicated the computer screen. "There is something on here you need to see."

"On the computer?" As she spoke, the power flicked back on, and the computer beeped and stuttered into life.

"How do you know what a computer is?" she asked. "They don't have them where you come from."

He held his hand over his good eye. "I see much in here," he said. "I see everything." He leaned over and, with a click of the mouse, opened the webcam program. "Sit down," he said, grasping her wrist and pushing her gently into the chair.

Sara did as she was told, then saw that there was a new file marked 'unwatched' waiting in the menu. She clicked on it, and it opened up. The video began to run. This living room, soft music playing. It was Coldplay, Dillon's favourite. A knock at the door. Then Dillon moved past the camera to answer it. The low resolution of the webcam was unkind to his face, making his cheeks look hollow.

"What is this?" Sara asked.

A firm hand on her shoulder pinned her to the seat. "Just watch."

Voices off-screen. "Hello, Dillon."

"Emily!" Puzzlement, tenderness.

"Can I come in?"

"Of course you can."

Then, standing in front of the webcam, was Emily Pascoe. Sara's erstwhile college friend. Dillon's lost love.

"What the . . . ?" Sara gasped. The lining of her heart began to glow with heat.

"Where is Sara?" Emily asked.

"Away on business. She'll be back tomorrow night. Do you want to sit down?"

"No, I won't."

Sara's senses prickled.

"Can I ask why you're here?" Dillon's shoulder was turned away from the camera, but Sara could see in his muscles that he still wanted Emily Pascoe. That he had never stopped wanting her. "I never thought I'd see you again."

Emily fixed him in her sultry gaze. "Dillon, I hear you're getting married."

"I am. Next month."

"But you and I, we have unfinished business."

Sara tensed. She waited for Dillon to deny it, to tell her that no, he was over her, that Sara was the soulmate whom he loved madly.

"Yes," Dillon said, all the slump and surrender of capitulation in his voice and body. "We do."

Emily's eyes grew dewy. She touched his shoulder, ran her fingers down his arm to his wrist. "I don't want to stop you getting married. I

35

just want to feel your arms around me. I want you to take me against your body, just once. Then we can get on with our lives. Nobody will ever know."

Damn him. He didn't even waver. "Yes," he said. "Oh, yes."

Odin's hand tightened on Sara's shoulder. Protectively.

Emily cleared her throat loudly, stepping back. "I'm so thirsty. Could you fetch me a drink?"

"Of course." Dillon, under her spell now, hurried away. "Sit down, make yourself comfortable," he called. "I'll be . . . I'll be right back."

But before his sentence was finished, Emily had turned to the camera, dissolved and reconfigured. In her place was Odin, looking directly at Sara with a sad expression. Then he slipped out of shot. The sound of the front door closing.

Dillon returning with a glass of water. One of the glasses Sara and Dillon had bought together when they'd first moved in with each other. "Emily?" he said, puzzled. Forlorn.

The video flickered to black.

Sara could only hear her heart, beating fast but thready. Beating only because it had to.

"As I was saying, before you interrupted me," Odin said, quietly and darkly from behind her shoulder. "Dillon Kincaid failed the first test and now he has failed the second."

The grey descended and covered everything, like fog on an autumn morning. Sara hid her feelings: it was her most practised talent after all. She smiled and laughed and spoke and ate and showered and slept, but only an inch deep. Underneath the Sara that the world saw, was the Sara who had crumpled in on herself as though made of thin cardboard.

It seemed the wedding was a great machine made of cast iron cogs that turned perpetually. Inescapable. She needed a year or two to decide if she would stay with Dillon, but she had only a few more weeks. Emotional paralysis. She didn't decide to stay, she just couldn't decide to leave.

The wedding would go ahead as planned. Sometimes she told herself, perhaps he wouldn't have betrayed her completely. Perhaps he would have said this isn't right, you have to go, I love my fiancée.

But she knew. She'd always known. She was his second choice.

At night, in her dreams, she looked for Dillon. She wanted to see him come wading across the river. She searched every face for his eyes, his nose, his lips. She thought if she could tear him to pieces in her dream, then the anger would dissolve. The jealous lurch of her stomach would settle. She would be able to get on with married life.

But he was never there.

This is new, she thinks, as she becomes aware she is dreaming but there is no hall, no river, no forest of spears. The sky is deep velvet blue and she can see so many stars that her breath catches in her throat. Everything is caressed with grey-white starlight. Her bare feet are on dewy grass. Ahead of her there is a cliff, and a man sits on the edge of it. It is Odin.

She approaches. "Father? Is this a dream?"

He turns, pats the place on the grass next to him. "No. I needed to talk to you. Sit."

Sara sits. She feels the load fall from her shoulders as she leans into his hefty arm. She hangs her feet over the edge of the cliff. Below them is a raging sea, crashing and crashing on rocks. Colossal wildness, undreamed of, making her veins thrum. "Where are we?"

"Bifrost. The way between." He raises his hands and a rumble gathers across the sea. It sucks all the ambient sound out of the night, creating a vacuum in her ears. Then the deafening wail of a horn snaps the air. Sara covers her ears. Immense coloured lights unribbon into life in front of her. It is the aurora, viewed from above, and she can see that it is, indeed, a bridge, leading off to a mist-shrouded place miles and miles distant. The horn abruptly stops, leaving her ears ringing, but she can hear the low, throbbing pulse of the lights as they undulate gently.

Sara's heart squeezes. She is mortally sick of seeing existence through a pinhole.

A flapping noise drags her attention away from the lights. Two black shapes flying against the starlit sky.

"My ravens," Odin says, holding up an arm for them to land on. "Thought and Memory."

The birds land on his leather-clad arm and he chucks them under the beak, one after another, making a little clicking noise. Sara enjoys his display of tenderness.

"Go on now," he says. One bird takes off, then the other. They cross over, seem to become one. Soar up high, then plummet again, splitting back into two.

"Did you bring me here to show me all this?" Sara asks. Urgently, she hopes he will ask her to stay forever. The wedding will be off. She won't have to look at Dillon every morning and feel the pain of knowing he doesn't love her as much as she loves him.

"No," Odin says. "I brought you here to ask you whether you've decided to call off the wedding. He's failed two tests. Do you still intend to marry him?"

Sara hesitates, thinking of her mother's hands tying ribbons in her hair. Her mother who has raised her the best way she knew. Then she realises she shouldn't hesitate; she should speak quickly. "Of course," she manages. "I love him."

A sudden bitter coldness grips her. An icy wind shoots past, tangling her hair and covering her skin in gooseflesh. Then it is gone. A dark shadow passes over them. She tries to follow it with her eyes, but it has already disappeared out to sea. She is left with a mild trepidation that keeps a little breath trapped in her lungs with every exhalation.

"You love him?" Odin asks, as though the cold shadow hadn't passed. "Even though you know how little he values you."

"He values me. He really does. You don't understand him. I've always known how he felt about Emily. It was painful to see, but not a surprise."

"He does not value you enough, Sara. You are extraordinary. You have strength beyond mortal knowledge. You have Aesir blood. You can stride across the clouds and kill with a Viking's courage. He should worship you; you are so much greater than he is."

The pride in her power is buried deep, not allowed to shine. She is afraid to let it shine, and so she speaks aloud the words she has always spoken under her breath. "I just want a quiet life. I never asked for supernatural strength. It's been a burden, not a blessing." She puts her hand over his. "Please, can we stop this now? All this business with tests and so on? Dillon is a good man, he really is. I'll get over my jealousy and we'll have a nice life."

Odin's single-eyed gaze searches her face, then he sighs and turns to the mist at the end of Bifrost. "It's too late."

"Too late?"

"The third test has already started."

Dread like cold iron presses on her heart. She remembers the icy shadow that passed over them, headed out across the sea. "What have you done?"

Sara woke, confused in the dark. Her ears still ringing.

No, her ears weren't ringing. Her mobile phone was ringing. The digital clock told her it was one a.m. She'd gone to bed early, before Dillon was back from work at the warehouse. The other half of the bed was neat and cold.

She snatched up the phone. "Dillon?"

"Where are you?" he snapped.

"Home in bed. Where are you?"

"Home? Then why did you call me to come here?"

"Come where?"

"Sara, what the hell is going on?"

Her heart knocked on her ribs. "Dillon, listen carefully. I didn't call you. I've been asleep. Tell me where you are now. I think you're in danger."

"In danger?"

"Where are you?" she shrieked.

A quarter-moment of silence as her fear infected him. "I'm at an industrial estate out near the airport. You said you were here with a flat tyre."

The cage-fighting arena. It had to be. "Is there a green building? With a white banner?"

40

"Yes. It says, 'Blood Arena.'"

"Get in your car and come home. Now."

"Do you want to explain what's going—" An abrupt click. Three loud beeps. Then silence.

CHAPTER THREE

OUT OF THE CAGE

ARA WONDERED IF HE'D BE DEAD BEFORE she got there, but then remembered that Odin had made sure she witnessed every one of Dillon's failures. *I want you to see with your eyes.* She parked the Suzuki at a crazy angle out front of the arena and stepped out. The rumble of traffic in the distance. A shower of wintry rain, harsh across the aluminium roof of the arena. The thin glow of the streetlight half a block away. She grabbed the torch from her glove box.

The door was locked, so she kicked it, bent it double, then peeled it aside and went in. The arena was in darkness. She shone the torch around. Shadows retreated from it. Dillon paced the cage, alone.

"Dillon!" She ran down through the auditorium, past the rows of plastic seats to the centre. The room smelled of cold concrete and stale rum.

He raced to the gate. A padlock held it closed. He rattled it with all his strength. "What the fuck is happening, Sara?"

She swung her torch around, found a covered power box on the base of the cage. She hit every switch, hoping for light. Nothing.

Magic. They were covered in it. Whatever *they* were.

"Who put you in here?"

"I didn't see them properly, they covered my face. But they were big and . . ." He exhaled roughly. "I think I'm going crazy."

"What did you see?"

He blinked. Looked away, his hair falling across his eyes. "Monsters."

Sara's stomach went cold. "I'm going to get you out," she said.

"How?"

"I'm sorry you had to find out like this."

"Sara?"

She hefted the padlock in her hand, twisted it. The iron snapped like a dry twig. The gate swung open. "Come on, let's go."

Heavy, shuffling footsteps.

"How did you . . . ?"

"Go! Now!" Then she turned her face up to the roof and shouted, "Call them off! He can't pass! We both know he can't pass!"

Dillon's face twisted with angry sobs. "Stop it, Sara! Tell me what's happening." Stubbornly, he held onto the gate. Even the imminent threat of monsters couldn't convince him to trust her.

A deep shiver loosened her gut. Fear. Suddenly it was icy cold. She shone her slender beam of light into the dark auditorium, hardly able to focus. The rain intensified on the roof, drowning out her thundering heart. A shadow moved. Her skin puckered as the light hit the monster. Only it wasn't a monster, it was a man: seven and a half feet tall, with skin so white it glowed blue. He was dressed in cloth and leather; his long black hair gleamed. His eyes met hers, and they were so pale they looked white. The freezing menace in those white eyes loosened all her nerves from their sockets.

"Frost giant," she managed to say to Dillon, before the other three stepped out of the darkness. They formed a line and filed down towards the cage. The first one, the leader, raised his hand and indicated Dillon.

"No," Sara said. "Not him. Me." She turned to Dillon and, hands beneath his armpits, lifted him aside as though he were as light as a toddler. She strode into the cage.

"No! Sara!"

But the frost giants were racing towards her now, shoving Dillon roughly aside. The gate slammed shut. Dillon tried to open it again, but a blue-white charge leapt onto his fingers and knocked him backwards. He disappeared from the stage.

"Dillon?" She ran to the side of the cage and peered down. The chainlink was cold under her fingers. Her torchbeam found him lying on the ground. She didn't know if he was dead or just unconscious. She turned; dread lined her veins. Four of them surrounded her in a semi-circle. She ran her torch across their blue-white bodies. She couldn't tell them apart except that one wore a silver circle around his brow. He must be some kind of prince.

A breath. A pause.

One of the giants stepped forward and knocked the torch from her hand. It clunked to the floor and rolled to the side of the cage, caught by the chainlink. She had to fight them in the dark. Her soft, mortal body shuddered.

Sara closed her eyes and opened her arms. She remembered the dreams; her body filled with molten metal. She drew her elbows in and took a deep breath, then opened her throat and a shriek poured out of her: a tempest, a whirlpool, a piece of chaos. It echoed off the walls and ran like electricity across the ceiling. She opened her eyes, could barely see their shapes in the gloom, leaped and landed on the closest.

These creatures were nothing like the men she had fought at the river in her dreams. They were solid slabs of ice. Her knuckles split and bled as she punched him. Her opponent's blows were bruising, dazing, rattling her eyes in their sockets. But she hammered and hammered at his head until he started to crumple. They fell to the ground together. The thin reflection of blue-white torchlight turned everything into fast black shadows. Two of the others tried to haul her off him, but not before she had stamped and hammered his head to a squishy, bone-splintered paste beneath her knees and fists. One seized and held her while the other punched her. He ploughed fists into her stomach and she held it tight as cold steel against the blows. The final one, the prince with the dully gleaming silver circlet, hung back watching. These were his underlings. They would soften her up so he could take her more easily. She had to get away from them and get her hands around the prince's neck, or she wouldn't survive.

She shrieked again, calling up the storm in her veins, muscles, sinews. The freezing iron clamps of their hands around her upper arms tried to pull her back, but she strained against them, shuffling forwards, until both of them lost their footing and were dragging behind her. She lifted her arms and shook hard. First one slipped off, then the other. The prince stepped forward and, in a black moment, had her head in an arm lock.

With sudden white intensity, the electricity in the room burst back on. Everything looked hyper-real, over-exposed. Music. '*Tie a yellow ribbon round the old oak tree.*' The red floor made her eyeballs ache. She struggled against the prince but the other two were crowding in now. One punched her ribs, the other her head. A mad blur of fists and blood and black hair and bright colours. Her heart pumped wildly. The pain cracked through her body. She could taste her own blood. Helpless, desperate, descending under thick water.

I am Odin's daughter. I am not weak. I do not surrender. I will be all that I can be.

Thudding blows. Ringing ears.

I can stride across the clouds and kill with a Viking's courage.

"Sara?" Dillon's voice, a long way off.

Pulling every shred of strength from every nerve and fibre of her body; pulling it out from behind shame, from behind fear; sending it rocketing up into her arms, down into her legs.

One. Sara flexes her spine, breaking the prince's hold. He stumbles, uncertain on his feet a moment. Two. She turns and heaves the other two over. They land in a heap on the floor. Three. She raises her knee and slams her heel into their heads, one, the other, one, the other. Four. She rounds on the prince, flings herself at him, brings him down to the ground. Pins him, pummels him, teeth and claws in his neck and shoulders. A blur of black and thorns and blood and breath and madness and taking him apart, taking pieces of him apart between her palms and thumbs and shrieking, shrieking, screaming all of the screams of the primal abyss . . .

Five.

Five. Breathe. Breathe.

Sara sat back, realised she had the prince's head in her hands. She let out a shout of revulsion and dropped it on the ground.

"Oh, my God."

Sara turned, saw Dillon on the other side of the cage, watching her. In that moment, she saw herself through his eyes. His quiet, compliant Sara, sitting astride a headless frost giant, among torn and bloody bodies.

"Don't look at me," she said, spitting blood through ragged lips.

But he couldn't look away.

Later, much later, they finally spoke of it. The bodies had turned to ice and melted into water. They brought their cars home. They showered. Sara tended to her wounds alone in the bathroom, with the door shut. Dillon sat, awake and upright like a coiled spring, in their bed. The warm, soft bed where they talked and slept and made love.

"Dillon?" she said, dressed now in the pale lilac dressing gown Mother had given her for her birthday.

He seemed to shake himself. "Are you okay?" he asked.

"Bruised," she replied. "A little stiff."

"I should take you to hospital."

"No need. I'm not . . . built like other women. They didn't break anything." She perched on top of the covers next to him. "I'm sorry I never told you. I thought I could go my whole life without telling you."

"What are you? What were those things?"

She chose her words carefully. Dillon couldn't handle too many details. The very simplest brushstrokes were necessary. "My father is Odin, the Viking god. I have supernatural strength. The monsters came for you and would have killed you. They won't come back now. Odin has proven his point. I don't want to be strong, I want to be normal. I've hidden it my whole life, and I can go on hiding it. You'll never see it again. I promise."

Dillon's face worked. Eyebrows twitching, jaw clenching. "I can't un-see," he said.

"You might forget in time."

"You ripped his head off. You looked . . . crazy."

The shame of it, the weight of squirming embarrassment that he had seen her like that, made her angry. "Well, you said yes to Emily Pascoe," she snapped.

His pupils shrank to pinpoints. "How did you . . . ?"

Stalemate. They studied each other in the light from the open bathroom door.

Finally, she said, "Are we still getting married? I'll forgive you if you forgive me."

Dillon rubbed his hands over his face. Outside, the first birdsong in the birch wood. "Are you going to do that again? Ever? If I make you my wife?"

"No. No, of course not." Her heart beat fast.

He dropped his hands, fixed her in his gaze. "Who else would have us?" he sighed. "It's too late now."

The string quartet played Debussy, and the music floated on the spring breeze over the park and towards the birch wood. The sun shone, but from a long way off. Winter's chill still in the air. But no rain, and enough of the sweet smell of flowers blooming to make people smile and say, "A perfect day for a wedding."

A perfect day for *her* wedding. Sara breathed as deeply as she could against the restricting laces of her pale pink gown. She paced the small wooden deck behind the rotunda, her veil tickling her face.

Mother stopped her, grasped her hands. "Stop pacing. Everything will go just fine. Just a few more minutes."

"Is everyone here? What time is it? Is Dillon here?"

"Everyone's here. Including some people I've never seen before. But it's best for the bride to be a little late."

Sara tingled with curiosity. "People you've never seen before?"

"There's a very uncouth looking fellow up the back."

"Big beard? Eye patch?"

Mother nodded. "I presume he's a friend of Dillon's family."

"Yes," Sara lied. "He's an . . . uncle."

"He looks like a bikie." Mother smoothed Sara's veil. "All right, my darling. Deep breath. It's your special day."

Sara forced a smile. Her whole body tingled. Odin was here. She hadn't seen him in the month since the battle with the frost giants. She didn't know if he was proud of her or disappointed in her. She desperately wanted to know.

The bridal march started. The breeze freshened. Treetops rattled. Mother looked towards the birch wood with a slight frown. "They really should cull that wood," she said.

Sara's veil whipped against her throat. She followed Mother through the rotunda. Mother adjusted Sara's hem then fell behind her. Matron of Honour. They started down the short paved path between the rows of plastic seats. Head down. She stole a sideways glance. There was Odin, his own head bowed. Her breath was caught between her ribs.

She walked down towards where the celebrant stood with Dillon and his best man. Dillon smiled. She could see it was forced. He kept reassuring her that they had their whole lives to deal with their problems, but he hadn't kissed her or made love to her since the third test.

The music stopped. A hush fell. The celebrant began to speak. The wind again, fresh and high and too cold for spring. Sara risked another glance towards Odin.

He was gone.

The space between her ribs grew heavy and chill. He was gone. And why should he not go? She had made her choice. She had turned her back on her supernatural ability, she had decided to marry the man who failed every test her father had set. She had chosen to forgive Dillon his infidelity, so that he could forgive her violent secret.

Only that wasn't fair, was it? She had known it from the moment she had said it. His sin was weakness; hers was strength. And strength was not a sin. It had *never been* a sin.

The wind picked up her veil, whipped it aside and off her face, half-pulled the diamanté comb from her tortured hair. Sara plucked it from her head and dropped it on the ground. It went tumbling off across the grass. Her hair fell loose. She breathed, she closed her eyes. She could hear their eyebrows lifting. The celebrant paused.

"Sorry," Sara said to the celebrant, opening her eyes. "Please continue."

Dillon watched her closely. She tried to smile and found she could only bare her teeth. He recoiled, almost imperceptibly. Her heart thudded hard in her throat.

"Do you, Dillon Kincaid, take Sara to be your lawful wedded wife . . . ?" The vow rang on like a cloud passing over the sun.

"I do," Dillon said, warmth flushing his voice. "Yes, I do."

"Do you, Sara Jones . . . ?"

Sara tried very hard to listen to every word, to know exactly what she was swearing to. But a black shadow caught her eye. She glanced up.

Two ravens, weaving in patterns above. She watched them, her heart lifting and falling. Her blood pulsing audibly.

She became aware of a silence. She startled, looked back at the celebrant. At Dillon. It was time for her to speak.

To swear.

To say, "I do," to Dillon and "I don't," to . . . everything else.

The ravens darted past overhead. Black wings against the pale blue sky. Disappeared into the birch wood.

Sara touched Dillon's hand, all her sorrow leaden in her fingertips. "I can't," she said.

The wind became suddenly furious. There were alarmed cries as guests held onto their hats. The treetops swirled wildly, and Sara strode away, across the park. Then she kicked off her shoes and ran, hard, heart pumping, towards the woods.

"I'm coming, Father," she said under her breath as branches caught and tore the pink lace of her dress. Louder. Calling. "Father! Odin! I am coming! I am becoming!"

And all her body and being bent towards him, as she had been trying to do her whole life.

II THE CITY AND THE SQUARE

'I am called Wanderer, Warrior and Helm-
wearer . . .

. . . you know I am Odin—Come close to me
now, if you dare.'

—*Grimnismal*

CHAPTER ONE

ODIN'S
CHALLENGE

AWAY FROM HER OLD LIFE AND INTO
the uncharted future, Sara Jones followed her
father's ravens. Stones and broken branches
punched her bare feet as she ran. The birds fluttered ahead of her.
Sometimes they landed on a branch a hundred feet away, inky black
in the shivering forest. Other times they disappeared from view
altogether and she ran on in hope and fear until she heard their clattering wings again.

She could smell the dank odour of the river and knew the chase
must end soon. The birds waited on a low birch branch. Sara drew
close, slowed to a walk, eyes fixed on them. One kept its gaze on her,
the other clacked its beak against the knotted wood.

"Where is he?" she asked.

But they shot up, up and out through the canopy, and she lost sight of them. Panting, she pushed her body forward again, but she was running out of forest. She burst out into pale white afternoon light. At the edge of the forest, where it met the swampy edge of the river, a crumbling pier jutted out into the gunmetal water. The ravens perched on the birdshit-spotted railing, close to the far end. As soon as her feet struck the wooden boards, they took to the sky.

Up and away, and down the snaking river towards the City.

Sara stopped running.

She couldn't run on water. She couldn't fly. Her father's gift of supernatural strength was great, but not much use in chasing ravens. Sara watched as the black shapes disappeared into the distance. The sun caught in the windows of the tall buildings, and they gleamed like fabled towers. The distance stole their detail and made them beautiful. But she knew the City and it wasn't beautiful. In there, on the ground, it was grimly dark and sharp fumes infused the stone and dank alleys. Living in the Square meant she had never had to go to the City. The bright white mall had everything she needed, and her job had been at a low office block among other low office blocks in a gated park where the sound of the pruning saw was as common as the sound of the espresso machine. Sara's heart squeezed tight at the thought of it; she wouldn't be going back to the Square. All of the ordinary certainty of her old life was gone.

Odin was in the City, so into the City she must go.

Sara walked the edge of the river until she came to the junction between the Square and the slightly less well-heeled suburb that abutted it. By now, the afternoon shadows grew long and the chill had deepened. She made her way along suburban streets to a main road, past birdbaths and garden gnomes and low fences and yapping dogs and many, many red roofs. Ahead, across four lanes of traffic, she saw a bus shelter. The ashphalt was warm under her feet, holding on to the day's sunlight. A young man sat at the stop, white headphones jammed in his ears as he played a game on his mobile phone.

"Excuse me," she said, tapping his elbow.

He looked up, took in her appearance and recoiled a little. Bare feet, torn lace dress, wild hair. He popped out one of the headphones and waited for her to speak.

"Does this bus go to the City?" she asked.

He nodded warily.

"I don't have any money. I don't have . . . anything," she said, and her voice caught but she didn't cry. She wouldn't cry.

His wariness turned to empathy. "No problem," he said, and he put his hand in his pocket and found two coins, which he gave to her. "Sorry, I don't have anything to give you for the return journey."

"There is no return journey," she said, and sat next to him. "Thanks."

As the bus made its way to the City, Sara's mind kept returning to the other life that she had run from. She'd be married by now: Mrs Sara Kincaid. Perhaps they would still be taking photographs in the park. Or perhaps by now they would have made their way to the small restaurant they had booked out. She could be riding the happy buzz of cold champagne, with Dillon on her arm, surrounded by music and family. At thoughts of her mother, Sara closed her eyes, leaned her forehead on the glass. When she opened them again, the light had started to bleed from the sky. The bus crossed the bridge into the City.

The spare change she had borrowed only took her two zones, so she had to step off the bus at the interchange on the western side of the City. Trains rumbled underground. She stood for a moment at the junction of two busy streets and searched the sky for ravens. Nothing. The sun had slipped low, and the first of the evening chill prickled across her bare arms. She hugged herself.

What if she never found him?

No, she wouldn't give up and go home on the first day. His ravens had definitely come towards the City, and that meant he was here somewhere. Maybe she didn't need to find him. Maybe he would find her.

She couldn't stand forever on the cold street corner in a torn wedding gown. She looked up. Sharp shiny hotel buildings towered over the transport interchange, but none of them would take her in. She began to walk along the street. Her best hope was a small hotel desperate for the business, who might give her a night's accommodation on the security of her engagement ring.

On an exhaust-blackened alley around the corner from a fast food restaurant, she found The Inchcolm, a six-storey hotel that hadn't seen fresh paint in forty years. She walked into the dim foyer and waited at the scarred counter for a plump, red-faced man to end his phone conversation. He was in no hurry. Sara glanced around. Two vinyl chairs and a dusty plastic potted palm. A desk with a chunky PC on it, under a sign that said *Internet $3 for 30 mins*. Clean but grim.

"Can I help you?"

She turned at the sound of his voice. "I need to stay . . . I'm not sure how long. I can't get my credit card until later in the week, but I can give you this for now." Sara slid off her engagement ring and placed it on the counter in front of him.

His gaze jumped from the ring to her face with amusement. "Did you run away from a wedding?"

"Yeah," she answered.

"Your own?"

She nodded.

"Is he going to come here looking for you and bust up my stuff?"

"He has no idea where I am, and he's not the kind of man to bust things up."

He shrugged, pushed a form across the counter for her. "I'm going to need to eyeball that credit card within seventy-two hours. Got it?"

Seventy-two hours. Would she have found Odin by then? Maybe he'd have taken her with him to Asgard. The world of hotels and credit cards and engagement rings seemed very small. "Yeah, got it," she said, scribbling in the number and signing the form. "Can you send some food up?"

"Kitchen is only open for breakfast."

"I'll pay you triple."

"Bacon and eggs okay?"

She thought about her wedding dinner, how her mother had agonised over it. "Sara, the only right way to do this is to offer a chicken dish *and* a beef dish. Some people don't like red meat."

"Bacon and eggs is fine," she said.

"Give me half an hour." He handed her a key. "Fourth floor. Room 409. The lift's not working, but you don't have any luggage."

"Thanks," she said, and made her way up the stairs.

The room was tiny, dim but clean. A door led to a bathroom where the smell of rose-scented soap was so strong it made her eyes water. Dark wood panelling and brown blankets. In a cupboard she found a kettle and a perfunctory mini-bar. The supermarket price tag hadn't been picked off the bag of chips she opened. She made instant coffee, ate chips, took a hot shower in a pink enamel tub, then pulled her wedding dress back on. This time she didn't bother with the laces. She switched on the television, but her mind couldn't focus on anything. It kept skipping and slipping, so she went to the window and tried to find the sky with her eyes. A small wedge of starless darkness between buildings. No birds. Too late in the day for birds now.

She looked down. A harsh security light illuminated industrial bins and empty milk crates. On the edge of the light stood a man. She frowned. It wasn't Odin. Nowhere near as large and colourful. This man's hair was long and white blond, a gleaming contrast against the dark grey and brown clothes he wore. He had a blond beard, too, divided into two plaits. She thought at first that he was in some kind of costume: thick winter boots, a brown cloak over grey shirt and pants. But his clothes looked too lived in, too worn to be fancy dress. She watched him for a moment, and then he turned and looked up and she was sure he was looking directly at her.

Sara took a step back from the window. Had a friend of Dillon's followed her? Had her mother already hired a private detective? But then she realised there was no way he could see in. She had seen the hotel from the outside, and the windows were mirrors from the alleyway. Sara returned to the window and watched him a while. It was uncanny, the feeling he was gazing back at her. He had a strong face, with a large nose and a broad jaw. At length, he turned his back again, seemed to gaze at something else a while in the dark.

At that moment, there was a loud knock at the door. Her bacon and eggs had arrived. She sat on the bed with the wooden tray and ate eagerly. It was only when she was putting the tray aside on the tiny dresser that she remembered the blond man. She returned to the window, but he wasn't there. The alleyway was empty.

She sat on the bed, lay down on her side, and watched a cooking show and cried a while. The welcome dark of sleep descended.

When she woke, neck crooked, the imprint of the lace on her upper arm, something was different. The television was off. The lamp was off. She hadn't turned them off.

She sat up, aware of a hulking presence in the room. Her father, sitting in the dark next to the dresser, waiting for her to wake up.

"How long have you been there?" she asked.

"Just a few moments," he said.

She brushed her hair off her face. "How did you get in?"

He shrugged, didn't answer. Perhaps he used magic, or perhaps he simply picked the lock. He was right not to answer. It didn't matter.

"I left him," she said. "I left them all. To be with you." Even as she said it she felt the nerves loosen in her stomach. He was a stranger to her mind and heart; she only knew him in her blood. But her blood longed for Asgard.

Odin seemed to sense her fear. "The things you will see, my girl, when you cross Bifrost with me," he said gently.

"Do I need shoes?" she asked.

"We aren't going yet." As he spoke, the lights surged back on, the television crackled to life.

Sara picked up the remote control and switched it off. She studied him a few moments in the light. Even though his red-gold beard was streaked with grey and his forehead and eyes lined with age and wisdom, there was an essential vitality about him that meant he didn't seem old. He seemed eternal. "When are we going, then?"

"You need to prove yourself worthy of Asgard."

"I do? I thought I was your—"

"My daughter, yes, but there are others that reside there. Others who will not be so easily convinced you belong. It's better this way. Once you have proven yourself to them, nobody will dare to gainsay me."

Sara remembered fighting the frost giants. Her body stung at the memory. "What more do I have to do to prove myself?"

"The frost giants weren't yours to fight."

"Of course they were. I couldn't let them kill him."

"Yes you could have."

Somewhere in the next street a security alarm went off, ringing out its plaintive song in the night. Sara could hear traffic, rumbling trains at the interchange. Odin was silent a long time, as though he was still deciding what he would ask her to do for him. At length, he said, "I will release seven creatures of Asgard in the City. Once you have defeated them all, I will come for you."

Seven. She wanted to tell him that this wasn't fair, that she'd already done enough. But she knew he wouldn't be convinced otherwise. He'd already given his reasons. "How do I find them?"

"Like will find like."

Sara remembered the blond man she'd seen down in the alley. "Have you sent them yet? I saw a man, dressed strangely, outside. I had the impression he was looking for something, maybe even looking for me."

But Odin was already shaking his head. "No, I haven't decided who they will be or when they will come yet," he replied. "But I promise you at least a little warning." He smiled. "And yes, you will need shoes."

She looked down at her bare toes, the shell-pink toenail polish that her mother had painted on them. Thoughts of Mother aroused heavy feelings.

"Make no mistake," Odin said, "these challenges will be difficult. You must be very certain you want to come to Asgard."

"I can't go back to how things were," she said. "Living half a life."

"Less than half," he said.

"But will I be able to come back here sometimes? To visit?"

"You will be free to do as you please, but it is better to forget your life here. Thought and memory work differently in Asgard. A handful of days may seem to pass, but it will have been a handful of years on Midgard. You'll forget it for long periods, then seek it out again and find all that you love is dead and cold underground." He placed his palm over his eye-patch. "I see it all, in here. I am master of thought and memory, but I gave up my eye to have that ability. Your Aesir skills are in strength and courage, not in wisdom. When you leave, it will be very difficult to come back."

Sara nodded. He was right; she was not wise. She had never been a good thinker. The sadness she felt was acute, but not enough to convince her to stay. "All right, then, I accept your challenge."

His beard split with a grin. "Good girl." He stood. "I look forward to bringing you to Valhalla," he said. "I will stand next to you proudly."

Her body filled with the thrill of longing. "I won't let you down."

Odin crossed the room and left by the door, closing it softly behind him. The security alarm abruptly stopped, leaving a vacuum of silence pressing against her ears. Sara turned on the television, too excited to sleep now, and watched old movies until dawn.

Sara knew she stood out: tall and ungainly in her wedding dress and bare feet at the train station. She chose Monday morning rush hour to travel, hoping to get lost in the masses pouring through the concourse. A woman with two large suitcases struggled through the check-gate, and under the pretence of helping her, Sara managed to slip through without a ticket. She jumped on a train just before the doors slid closed, and stood between men in grey suits reading newspapers one-handed.

Her body was weary, so weary, and her eyes felt as though they'd been rubbed in grit. She had slept only a fitful hour or two before getting up and making her way down to the interchange. Her sleep had been jumbled with fragments of dreams. Dillon driving her car carelessly and wrecking it, then laughing about it. Walking through the infinite corridors of a department store looking for her mother. Fighting off seven supernatural creatures seemed impossible this morning. She simply wanted to get back to the hotel and sleep.

At the next three stops, the train disgorged most of its passengers, as they went to jobs in the City. Sara found a seat and watched out the window as the train headed into the suburbs. At Hospital Station she saw a ticket inspector get on, so she quickly opened the door and stepped off. She was around a mile from home.

No, not home. A mile from Dillon's home.

He would be at work. In the awful weeks leading up to the wedding, he had willingly given up his honeymoon leave to take up a new project at work. At the time she had been sad, offended. Had he thought he was marrying a monster, one who wouldn't appreciate a week by the ocean with sand between her toes?

Or would he be home, nursing a broken heart?

Sara almost laughed. No. She could all too readily see Dillon telling his friends, "I dodged a bullet there. She was weird." He wouldn't tell them what kind of weird; he would eventually convince himself it hadn't happened.

The morning sun was bright in their little courtyard garden. The parking space where she'd used to keep her little Suzuki was empty: Dillon had persuaded her to sell it the week before the wedding to pay off their credit cards. She had no house key, but the lock disintegrated in her fist easily enough. She pushed the door open and went inside. The smells and sounds were so familiar. The hum of the fridge, the tick of the kitchen clock, the lingering scent of toast and coffee.

No time for nostalgia, no time for regret. She ran up the stairs to their bedroom. One side of the bed unslept in. Dillon's tablet on the end of the bed. She swiped it into life, found the last thing he had been looking at this morning. Websites for home security systems. The day after his failed wedding, he had sat in bed and researched home security systems. He was afraid. Of her.

Sara unlaced the wedding gown for the last time, left it in a pool on the floor. She grabbed a suitcase, threw in t-shirts, underwear, pull-overs, jeans, and warm dresses. She pulled a long navy dress on, a pair of flat-heeled boots. Threw toiletries into the suitcase and retrieved her handbag from the hook behind the bedroom door. Took her mobile phone from the bedside table and wound up the charger. It had been switched off since before the wedding, and she had no desire to switch it back on.

She paused a moment, looked around. Was there anything else she needed?

Her eyes lit on the framed photograph on her dresser. Sara and Mother, ten years ago, on a trip to the beach. Sara had been an awkward teenager, spotty and too eager to smile. Mother was immaculately coiffed and made-up, despite the fact that she was poolside at a beach resort. Palm trees and sarongs, heads leaning together. They looked nothing alike.

Sara picked up the photo and slid it into her suitcase, then left their house for the last time.

As she rode the train back to the City, she began to wonder how long it would take for Odin to send her his seven monsters. A week, a month, a year? How long would her credit card last? Had Dillon already frozen their joint account?

She turned the problem over while she trundled her suitcase over the uneven pavement between the interchange and her hotel. A handwritten sign on fluorescent pink paper on a black door caught her eye. *Help Wanted. Good Rates, Cash Payment. Apply Within.*

Sara stood back and read the switched-off neon sign over the door. *Ally's Alley. Bar and Nightclub.* Barmaid work wasn't beneath her. She could pour beers and make cocktails if, at the end of it, she could leave Midgard behind. Sara pushed the door open, pulling her suitcase behind her.

The room was dark and cavernous, and smelled of old smoke and beer-soaked carpet. Sara glanced around but couldn't see anyone. A door behind the bar was open, and she saw weak daylight beyond it. "Hello?" she called.

No answer. She left her suitcase by a high table and ventured behind the bar. "Hello?"

"Out here!" came the answer.

Sara found herself inside a cement room with metal shelves, stacked with wooden crates. A back door was open onto the access road behind, and there she found a tall woman struggling with a stack of crates and kegs. The woman looked up. She was dark-skinned, her hair in long dreadlocks, and she wore a lime green jump suit. Sara guessed she was between forty and fifty.

"Hi, I'm Sara," she said.

"Ally," she replied, head tilted curiously.

"You own the bar?"

"I own the bar. And if the driver refuses to take the delivery in, then I have to. Nobody else is going to do it." She snorted a cynical laugh, hefting a crate and shuffling into the storeroom. "This is the last thing I thought I'd be doing today."

"Same," Sara said, following. "Why did he refuse?"

"Some health and safety rubbish. I preferred it back in the good old days, when men were men." She slid the crate onto the shelf with a thump. Bottles rattled inside. "How can I help you?"

"I saw your sign. I'm looking for a job."

"Ah. Sorry, but no."

"No? You already have someone?"

"No. I should have been clearer on the sign. I need security. You know, a bouncer."

67

"Oh." Sara hesitated. Why not? She had the strength. Mother wasn't here telling her to hide her ability anymore. "Actually," she said. "I could do that job."

Ally turned and looked her up and down, her lips twisted in a dubious expression. "I don't think so." She headed back outside, Sara behind her.

"Really, I'd be good at it," Sara said.

"No offence, and it pains me to say this, but you're a girl."

Sara hesitated a moment as Ally returned her attention to moving the crates. Behind them were several aluminium beer kegs.

"Ally?" she said.

"You still here?"

"Are those kegs full?"

"Yeah, why?"

"Watch this." Sara walked to the nearest keg, scooped it up under one arm, and carried it to the store room as easily as another woman might carry a yoga mat.

Ally called out behind her. "You're hired. Can you start Wednesday night?"

In the coldest point of the early morning, Sara woke, flushed with fear. The unfamiliar room seemed hostile. Where was Dillon? Where was her pillow and quilt and the familiar sounds and smells of her house?

She sat up and hugged her knees. She'd left the curtains open, and the security light in the alley reflected off the wall opposite, lending a wash of grim yellow light to her room. Slowly her heartbeat returned to normal. She lay back down and closed her eyes.

As she drifted off, an image formed behind her eyelids. Burning runes. She opened her eyes and they disappeared, closed them again and the strange letters were back. Sara drifted off, the indecipherable word still burning against her vision.

CHAPTER TWO

TROLLS AND
WITCHES

BY ELEVEN P.M., ONLY A FEW DOZEN people had passed in and out of *Ally's Alley*. Most of them had looked her up and down, taken in her black t-shirt with SECURITY written on it, and walked by her with a puzzled expression. One young drunk man had made a joke about "the chick bouncer" but it wasn't offensive enough to kick him out. And how she wanted to kick someone out. The unleashing of her power was thrilling beyond imagination, and she'd spent most of her life reining it in.

A band set up, played a half-hearted set, then went to sit despondent at the bar. Ally, who was in fluorescent pink tonight, didn't seem concerned about the lack of customers.

"It hots up closer to midnight," she said.

Sara stifled a yawn and leaned against the wall by the door.

Ally was right. By eleven-thirty the crowd began to swell. Noise and cigarette smoke. The girls behind the bar moved from one customer to the next with smile-free proficiency. The band returned to the stage and found energy in the audience's enthusiasm. It wasn't the kind of music Sara liked—far too bland and FM-friendly—but she found herself tapping her foot along with it nonetheless.

With the increased crowd came an increase in heat and drunkenness. Sara's skin began to twitch. Something would happen soon, surely. Two young men took their beers onto the dancefloor and Sara had to tell them to move before they spilled their drinks; but they simply apologised and did as they were told. A girl began shrieking at her boyfriend, but was quiet the moment Sara approached.

None of these people were *wild* enough.

Back to her spot by the door, watching the crowd, waiting.

Around one in the morning, an altercation broke out near the bar. It seemed one man—a tall, slender one with dark hair—had been jostled by the crowd and spilled his drink on another man. The tall man had a hard time apologising over the screaming tirade of curses coming from the other, much stockier man, so Sara started making her way over just in case.

In less than a second, the stocky man had taken the tall man in a headlock. The tall man began to kick wildly, and a chair went flying, knocking over a table full of drinks. The crowd parted, Sara strode in.

"Get off him!" she shouted at the stocky man, who ignored her.

Her blood lit up.

"I said, get off him!" She grasped his forearms and wrenched them apart. He buckled under the pain, fell to his knees, but she yanked him back up and pulled him under her arm, then carried him to the entrance with his toes madly scrambling for purchase. With her spare arm she pushed the door open, letting in a blast of cold fresh air. She released him roughly, and he fell on his side on the pavement.

"You fucking freak!" he shouted at her, and she wanted to stomp him into the ground but didn't.

"I'll count to ten, and if you're not gone . . ."

He clambered to his feet and hurried off. Sara was almost disappointed.

She turned to see the tall man standing at the door. "Thanks for that," he said.

"No problem."

"I don't get into fights. I mean, I'm not that kind of guy. I just spilled my drink." He smiled, extended his hand. "I'm Ben."

She eyed his hand warily, then took it for a brief moment. "Sara," she said.

"Can I ask you something?" he said. "How did you do that? How did you just . . . it looked effortless. He must weigh twice what you do."

She shrugged. "That's my job," she muttered, then pushed past him and back inside.

The bar closed at three, and Sara was busy mopping up reluctant drunks while the band packed up and the bar staff left. Ally was the last person left behind the bar, the band were lugging their sound equipment out through the storeroom and into the alley, when the door banged open and a thing walked in.

A thing. The only way to describe it. Six feet tall, dressed in some kind of stinking animal pelt, a neck like a Christmas ham, a deformed head with huge ears melted onto the sides, and a lower jaw that protruded so far Sara could see its lower eye teeth. And they were more like tusks.

Because she'd been waiting all night for something to happen, because that one small altercation had been all the excitement she'd been granted, Sara saw the troll and smiled.

"Come on then," she said to it.

The troll lunged forward, knocking her to the ground. Ally screamed. Two of the band members approached then backed away quickly. Sara struggled out from underneath the troll and tried to stand, only to have the creature grab her around the knees. She fell forward, onto its back. It tried to stand, with her tight in a knee-lock, but she began to pummel its ribs with all the force she could find in her hands, and the creature stumbled forward, crashing her into a table. They both landed on the beer-soaked carpet. Sara quickly climbed to her feet and stamped on its left hand. The creature howled with pain. She bent over and locked its head between her arms, dragged it into a half-sitting position, and began to haul it towards the exit. It gurgled and spat, and Sara tightened her grip. She kicked open the door and flung him onto the pavement, just as she had with the stocky man earlier that night. The door swung shut with a bang, and she jumped on top of the troll, pinning its arms beneath her knees, and began to punch its head. Somewhere she heard bells, like church bells but not as sweet, ringing out of tune in the dark. Her vision swam and she clutched instinctively at the troll's collarbone to stop herself from falling . . .

A soft breeze fans apart the mist and through it, Sara sees a winding forest path. The trees are ancient and knowing, soaring into cloud, aerial roots dropping like petrified tentacles to the ground. The rocks are bright green with moss, and a deep smell of old rain and fertile soil pervades her senses. The breeze comes again, rhythmically, as though the forest has lungs and is breathing her in. She can hear water in the distance, falling from a great height. Pale, slanted sunlight tips on and off leaves as they shiver and shudder. The cool is a kind of sweet bliss on her skin. Ah, she thinks, home; it's over.

As suddenly as the image had impressed itself on her senses, it disappeared. Her fists were still moving without her conscious will, the troll's head lolled bloodily to the side. Then it disappeared. Winked out of existence as though it had never been. Her knees jerked against the cold ground, her fist landed in the pavement, cracking both concrete and her knuckles.

Her blood thundered.

The door flew open behind her. She turned to see Ally.

"Where did he go?" Ally said.

"Disappeared," Sara said. It wasn't a lie.

"He was a big ugly fellow, wasn't he?" Ally said, helping Sara to her feet. "Here, let's clean up that blood on your knuckles. What an eventful first night on the job you've had."

A big ugly fellow. Had Ally really not seen that it was a troll? Or had her mind simply decided to make sense of the impossible somehow? And what had the vision been? Remembering it now was as sweet as falling in love. A treasure in her heart.

Sara took a moment to gather herself before following Ally in. She looked up and down the street. No troll. She had won.

Six more to go.

74

The thought of sleeping was ridiculous. Her muscles buzzed and her blood tingled. She paced her room for a while, then stopped in front of the photograph of her and Mother. She had been trying the last two days not to think of Mother, how she might be feeling. Sara knew she couldn't go back, couldn't say goodbye. Mother's anger and grief was the only thing with the power to undo her resolve. But she was struck by a strong desire to be near her somehow.

She pulled on her boots and pullover and left the hotel room.

No trains ran at this time of night, but the circle bus, which would be full of drunk boys and shoeless girls finding a passage home, trundled past the interchange every half-hour. She waited in a pool of light at the stop. The streets were empty but for the occasional car flashing past. At length, the bus trundled along and she climbed on board and found a seat near the front. As the bus moved off again, something outside caught her eye. A fair man in dark clothes stood diagonally opposite the bus stop. She was almost certain it was the same man who had been watching her window, the first night in the hotel.

The walk to Mother's place was more than a mile. Her stepfather, Pete, had deliberately bought a house as far from the main road as he could. No bus fumes ever washed over the manicured orange trees that stood either side of the front gate.

Sara approached just before dawn, when the birds were chirping cautiously in the camphor laurels. The grass was silver with dew. Her breath made steam. She stopped opposite Mother's house and couldn't go any further. This was the end of the journey. Forever outside her mother's life.

She stood there a long time, until grey dawn broke. Then she turned and headed back to the main road.

Because the troll had come so soon after Odin's visit, Sara hoped the whole trial would be over quickly. But another seven days passed with no sign of mythological monsters. She forced herself to grow used to the late hours at the club, and by the end of the week she was all but nocturnal; sleeping with the blinds pulled against the cold shafts of daylight that speared between the buildings, then rising as the peak hour rush surged homewards and the sun set. Time seemed to have turned on its head somehow, nights and days slurring into each other messily.

The upset to her sleeping routine meant she didn't dream, or at least she didn't remember her dreams. But the following Wednesday, in the space between sleeping and waking, light fluttered across the inside of her eyelids. It shifted and resolved. Burning runes.

Again.

Sara woke with a start, opened her eyes. Stumbling out of bed, she reached for the hotel notepad and pen. Last time she had seen runes, it had been the day the troll came. It was a different word this time, and she was determined to capture it.

ᚺ ᛌ ᚦ ᚱ

She dropped the pen and gazed at the runes a long time. How was she to interpret them?

A knock at her door. The red-faced hotel manager, Neville, had taken to bringing her bacon and eggs at five o'clock every afternoon. He seemed to have grown fond of her.

She opened the door to him. "Hi," she said.

"Sleep well?"

"Weird dreams," she said. "Is the computer in the foyer working today?"

"Seems to be. You need to send that poor jilted fiancé of yours an email?" He winked, setting down her tray. "Bring that down with you when you come, love. Save me a trip."

"No problem."

She ate, showered, pulled on a warm dress, and tore out the piece of paper with the runes copied onto it. Neville was nowhere in sight as she left the tray on the scarred reception counter. The computer took an age to boot up, ticking and clacking. She drummed her fingers on the melamine desktop.

Finally, she had a browser open. She typed in "runes".

So many hits. She clicked through a few websites until she found one that seemed to have a direct translation from Old Norse runes to modern English letters. She transcribed the word.

Heithr.

What did that mean? She typed it into the search bar and got a few pages of anagram solving hints. The search engine asked her, "Did you mean *hither?*"

"Find what you're looking for?"

This was Neville, returned to his post behind reception.

She pushed the chair back and stood. "Not really. Here I'll give you the three dollars."

"Don't worry about it. You're the best customer I've had all year.

While you're online, give us a good rating on Trip Reviews, will you?"

"Sure," she said, sitting down at the computer again. "Can I print something?"

"Go on, then. It'll send to the printer back here."

She printed out the page of rune letters, because it also listed short meanings for each rune. Maybe she could figure out what the dream meant that way. She punched in a quick five-star review for Neville and the Inchcolm Hotel, and it stood out starkly against the one- and two-star reviews already in place. Neville made her a cup of coffee and she took it back up to her room.

Working with the rune descriptions didn't help either. Sara began to suspect the dream had simply thrown them up randomly. Soon it would be time to go to work, so she put the page aside and climbed into her work clothes.

Sara didn't know if the days were warming up but the nights were still cold. A light drizzle had started outside, and she shrank into her jacket and pulled up the hood. Car tyres hissed on the wet road beside her as she walked along. She felt for a moment as though she could see herself from the outside, and she barely recognised herself, her life. Falling into the unknown. She squared her shoulders and kept walking.

The club was warm. She hung up her jacket and took her customary position near the entrance, her back against the stucco wall, watching the room. It was band night, same as last Wednesday, and a handful of long-haired men were sound-checking their equipment.

Tuning, cracking one drum at a time, making "tch-tch" sounds in the microphones.

"Got any requests, darling?" the lead singer said, his voice amplified through the room.

It took her a moment to understand that "darling" was her. "You wouldn't like any of the songs I like," she said.

"Try me."

"Know any Gorgoroth?"

He shook his head, but then the drummer burst into a staccato solo and the rest of the lead singer's sentence was lost.

Ally brought her a bottle of water. "Guy at the bar is asking about you," she said.

Sara eyed the bar. "Which one?"

The tall one in the green t-shirt.

Sara recognised him. It was Ben, the man who had been involved in last Wednesday night's fight. "What's he asking?"

Ally smiled. "If you're single."

Sara's body went hot and cold at the same time.

"Are you?" Ally continued.

"Yeah. But I'm not looking. I just got out of a . . . pretty serious relationship."

"I'll tell him," Ally said, then leaned a little closer. "To be honest, it struck me as kind of weird. I mean, you *rescued* him last week. Damsel in distress, big strong hero . . . you know."

"Yeah, I guess it is weird. Or I'm weird. One of the two."

Ally punched Sara's arm softly. "You sure pack a wallop for a chick. Wish I could do that." Then she was off back to the bar.

The night wore on, the crowd started to swell, but Sara couldn't relax. She had the feeling Ben might be looking at her, and she didn't know how to hold her body. She wasn't used to being looked at. She'd met Dillon when she was so young, so she didn't know how to act when a man was admiring her in a bar: it had never happened before.

She was on her break, sitting in the store room on an upturned crate and eating a microwaved pizza pocket, when he came to find her.

"You're not supposed to be here," she said.

"Ally said it was okay."

Sara rolled her eyes. Ally was playing matchmaker.

"Sorry, I'll go if you want me to," he said.

"No, it's okay. Hi. How are you?"

"I'm great. I hoped you'd be here again. Do you work every Wednesday?"

"I work every day except Monday and Tuesday."

"Ah. I should have come back earlier then."

"Listen, I—"

"It's okay, Ally told me. Single but not looking."

"Sorry," she said. She looked down at her pizza pocket then back at him. "Well, this is awkward."

"I'm always awkward," he said. "It's kind of how I live my life."

She hauled an empty crate out from under the shelf beside her and offered it to him. "Sit down," she said.

He did as she said. "Have you always been . . . really strong?" he asked.

"Um . . . yeah. My mum didn't like it much."

"And your dad?"

"He wasn't around. He lived a long way away. A really long way away." She didn't like answering his questions, so she asked one of her own. "How about you? What do you do? What's your thing?"

"My thing? I'm a writer."

"Published anything?"

"Nothing you would have heard of. I mostly write for the internet. Citizen journalism. That kind of thing."

"I'll look you up. What's your surname?"

He smiled sheepishly. "Well, my surname is Fordham, but I write under a pseudonym. Benjamin Midnight."

Sara couldn't help laughing, and Ben laughed too.

"I know," he said. "It's lame. It seemed like a good idea when I started at seventeen."

"Well, Benjamin Midnight," she said, finishing off the last of her pizza pocket and wiping her fingers on a bar towel, "I have to get back to work."

"Listen, if you ever want to get a coffee . . . "

"Um, maybe. I'm probably going to move away somewhere else really soon."

"But you could still meet me for a coffee."

She shrugged. "Like I said. Maybe."

Then she went back to work, but she kept thinking about him. Maybe it was because he looked a lot like Dillon, with his puppy-dog eyes and his floppy dark hair. But that was insane. He wasn't Dillon and anyway she had no business thinking about men that way, especially men here on what Odin would call Midgard. She would be out of here soon. At least she hoped it would be soon. Life was on hold until then.

Even though Ally tried to send Sara home directly after her shift ended at two a.m., she hung around and helped close up. She didn't like the idea of Ally being here alone so late, because she couldn't be sure another troll wouldn't turn up just after she left. Fighting off creatures from Viking mythology was one challenge; the other challenge was making sure nobody else got hurt in the process. Together they emptied the taps and wiped all the benches and vacuumed the cigarette-scarred carpet, and finally Sara watched Ally set the alarm behind the bar and they hurried out the back door and double locked it.

"Thanks," Ally said, pocketing her keys. "You're the best security guard I ever had. But don't you have a home to go to?"

Sara shrugged. "Not really. Not just now."

Ally looked as though she might ask Sara more questions about her personal life, but then she stopped and her gaze went over Sara's shoulder. Sara's blood shivered, and she turned around, expecting to see the blond man again. It wasn't a man, it was a woman. She was petite, wearing a cape and hood that was pulled over her head, and leaning on some kind of a walking stick.

"Weird," Ally said.

"She's waiting for me," Sara said.

"You know her?"

"Yeah. I think so. Her name's Heithr." Sara turned to Ally, offered a shallow smile. "Friend of my dad."

"Enjoy yourself then." Ally jingled off down the alleyway to her car.

Sara spun round to face Heithr, but she was gone.

"Shit," she muttered under her breath, racing off down the alley after her. If she lost this one, how much longer would she have to wait for her to come back? She burst out into the street, and Heithr stood diagonally opposite. The rain had passed over, but the air smelled like earth and bitumen. "Hey!" Sara called.

Heithr lifted one arm and pushed her hood off. Sara had been expecting an old woman, but she was young, with a pretty pointed face and long frost-fair hair.

Sara checked for traffic then ran across the road. Heithr turned and ran as well, ducking down another alleyway.

Sara put on a burst of speed and bolted after her, but she was fleet of foot and always a hundred feet ahead, ducking around corners and across roads, her black cape swirling behind her, her staff tapping on the ground.

Through the city streets they ran, splashing over puddles and rattling past construction sites, negotiating their way around street sweeper trucks and beggars. On and on, until Sara could see that Heithr was leading her towards the Parklands. Dawn was a pale promise at the edge of the sky. Finally, Heithr stopped, in the middle of an astro-turfed play area, flanked on either side by a deserted swing set and a climbing frame, wet with the night's rain.

Sara stopped too. Caught her breath. Approached warily. Heithr flung off her cloak, to reveal robes of blue and white and strings of glittering glass around her throat. She held her staff out in front of her. Sara approached, slowly, expecting her to run again. She didn't. Her staff ran with blue fire. As Sara drew closer, she pulled it back in one hand, as though she intended to hit Sara with it.

Sara kicked the staff out of her hand and it landed twenty feet away. Heithr spread her arms and Sara took the opportunity to crash tackle her onto the astroturf. As she did, heat flared into life under her. Heithr had exploded into flames.

Sara leapt off, shouting from the pain in her burned hands. Her palms were raw and bloody. Where Heithr had lain was a blue-orange bonfire, curls of black ash spiralling off it at immense speed.

She stood back to watch. That had been easy.

Perhaps it had been too easy.

A voice behind her. A word from another language. Sara turned slowly. Heithr, whole and unharmed. This time, she ran at Sara, ploughing into her so hard that Sara was forced into the climbing frame. Sara tried to fight her off, but her hands were agony, and clenching them into fists was impossible. Heithr smashed her head against the bars until it rang. Sara hooked her elbows over the frame to brace her upper body, then pulled Heithr's legs off the ground with a kick. Heithr hit the ground, and Sara kicked her once, twice, then . . . *whoosh*. She was on fire again. Sara was still in her workboots so she kicked her opponent another two times, before the fire became too intense to stand next to.

Sara retreated to the wet grass, bending to press her hands against it, trying to cool the horrible pain. So, the witch could set herself on fire to avoid being finished off. That was hardly fair. Sara breathed deep a few moments, bracing herself against the pain. She didn't hear her opponent approach from behind, but she certainly felt the kick in the middle of her back. Now she was pinned to the ground, the hard end of Heithr's staff driven into her spine. She tried to struggle away, but a piercing heat shot out of the end of the staff and into her spine, running up towards her skull and out to her limbs, temporarily short-circuiting every rational thought she had. The pain.

Heithr had magic. Sara didn't have magic. She couldn't fight magic. She only had strength.

So use it.

She gritted her teeth and pushed her burnt palms against the ground. With a burst of might, she shoved her upper body up, dislodging the staff and knocking Heithr off her footing. Sara reached around and seized the staff, wrenched it from her opponent's hands, and began to crack Heithr around the head with it. Blood flew. Until, inevitably, Heithr caught fire again.

Sara stood back, held the staff tight. She turned slowly in a circle, waiting for the witch to reappear.

A moment later, the staff was being pulled out of her hands invisibly. Sara clutched it despite the pain, then a small flame flickered in mid-air, grew, and resolved into the figure of the witch, her hands on the staff. She said something to Sara in the strange, old language.

"No way, it's my stick now." She hauled it free, pulled back and whacked Heithr square in her pretty elfin face, then drew back to whack her again. In that second, Heithr's eyes—green as the forest—locked on to hers.

A grassy slope leads down to the fjord. The water is dark and still and deep, deep enough to drown the saddest truths. A tiny square cottage sits further up the slope. White smoke curls thinly from the roof. The shuttered windows are painted green. Inside, there will be comfort, cosy smallness. Out here is the wild stillness of the grey-green world. Cloud covers the sun. Rain shimmers across the slope, across the water, peppering the surface. A few more feet and she'll be out of the rain, by her fire, and this pain will be behind her . . .

Just as the troll had, Heithr disappeared.

Sara waited, staff at the ready. Seconds passed. They turned into minutes. Still she waited, tensed against Heithr's return. The place in her vision seemed to call to her, and she closed her eyes and willed to be there again. But the vision didn't come back.

And nor did the witch.

Sara made her way to the emergency clinic just as dawn rain started to fall. The City was waking up. Early commuters and utility vans, their tail-lights bright in the grey. The inside of the clinic was warm. Four other people sat in the drab waiting area on a mismatched set of brown and grey chairs under a poster warning about the dangers of binge drinking. Sara took her place and prepared to wait, but when the triage nurse saw the state of her hands, she was advanced up the queue and was with a young Indian doctor within fifteen minutes.

"How did you do this to yourself?" he asked.

"I picked up something hot."

"What did you pick up?"

"It doesn't matter."

He continued cleaning up her hands, but she could tell his curiosity was piqued. "Did somebody do this to you?"

"No. I'm just really clumsy."

"You know," he said, his voice dropping conspiratorially low. "You can tell the truth. There's no shame in being a victim of domestic violence, but if you don't tell anyone your situation won't change."

So he had her picked for a battered bride. She almost laughed. The idea of some Midgard man exercising his will on her through violence was ridiculous.

"Don't worry," she said. "I promise you this isn't domestic violence. I've never had a husband, or a boyfriend, or any man in my life who's been violent with me." No, Dillon always brought her to heel through shame, not with his fists. "I got into a fight. I get into a lot of fights."

He didn't meet her eye as he bandaged her hands. "Is that so? Well, as a doctor can I suggest you try to avoid them from now on?" He finished off and released her hands. "Come back tomorrow morning if you can. I'd like to check on the bandages."

"Sure," she said, but she knew she wouldn't be back. She had always healed quickly. "Thanks."

"Don't forget this," he said, handing her Heithr's staff, which she'd brought with her from the park.

"Thanks," she said again, tucking it under her arm.

As she was crossing the foyer, the door of another consulting room opened and the man from the bar, Ben, stepped out. They saw each other, stopped awkwardly. Then Sara kept walking, briskly away.

"Hey, wait up," he called, hurrying out onto the street after her. "What happened to your hands?"

"Were you following me?" she asked, stopping and rounding on him.

"No. No not at all. My brother is an emergency nurse. I drop in on him at the clinic a couple of mornings a week to see if there are any good stories . . . you know, for my blog." He pushed his glasses back up onto his nose. "I promise, I'm not following you. I'm not some creep. I'm not—" A truck roared past, drowning out the rest of his sentence.

"Whatever," she said.

"Wow, that walking stick is amazing. Where did you get it?" He reached for it, then drew back sharply. "Hey, is that human skin?"

She studied the staff in the light of day. She'd thought it covered in leather, but now realised he was right. "Of course not," she said,

87

vowing to herself to dump the staff somewhere she never had to see it again.

"Your hands?"

"None of your business."

"Fair enough," he said, raising his palms, backing away. "I didn't mean to offend you."

She watched him go, then took a detour on her way back to the hotel. Down to the river, the swanky end of town, where all the trendy eateries were opening up and brewing coffee. How she longed for a coffee.

She took the staff down to the boardwalk, then all the way out on one of the ferry pontoons, and dropped it with a splash in the water. The river was murky and brown. The staff sank without a trace.

Sara was sore and weary. She ordered a coffee and sat on the board-walk while the sun climbed in the sky, making her eyes sting.

Sara didn't go straight to bed when she arrived back at the hotel. She stopped at the computer in the foyer, booted it up, and searched for him. *Benjamin Midnight.*

It took her to a website, *The Midnight Post.* She scrolled through it, skimming the entries. It seemed Ben was a conspiracy theorist of some kind. He reported on alien abductions, stars who faked their own deaths, hauntings, secret societies, and he even postulated on the existence of werewolves and vampires. No wonder she had caught his eye with her superhuman strength. It wasn't sexual interest; he just loved freaks. At least she believed him now about his brother at the emergency clinic. Several times he cited a "source" who had witnessed cagey patients with strange injuries "not so easily explained by medical science", though most of them sounded to her easy enough to explain as sex adventures gone wrong.

She closed the computer down and sat back for a few moments in the early morning gloom. So did Ben actually believe in the existence of monsters? Or was his belief idle, hopeful, like so many here on Midgard who longed for there to be something bigger than the usual window they looked through?

She could have laughed. He had *no idea*.

CHAPTER THREE
QUEEN OF
THE SEWERS

DID THEY EVER THINK OF HER, those people from her old life? Sara wondered this often, told herself she had no right to wonder about it, and tried to get on. Her mobile phone had sat in the bottom drawer of the wonky dresser in her hotel room for weeks now, and any temptation to turn it on had quickly been overridden by anticipation of the painful messages she knew would be on there from Dillon, from her mother. But might there also be messages she needed to hear, that would assure her Midgard would miss her?

Sara circled the idea all afternoon, then through the night at work, then again in the early morning dark. She went to bed just before five in the morning, couldn't get comfortable on her pillow, couldn't fight the impulse that she should turn the phone on and see what was on it.

Finally, she rose. Sat on the end of her bed in the dim light, and switched it on.

It took a few moments to find itself, then the SMS messages began to download. Over and over in her hand, it vibrated and tinged. They were all from Dillon. She scrolled through them, her face illuminated by the tiny screen.

I know you've been here don't come back u freak.

Fkn bitch u owe me a diamond ring.

What the hell are you anyway?

On and on it went. She noted the time and date they'd been sent, and could see that he'd sent fewer and less frequent texts as the days had passed, and they'd become gentler and gentler as his anger and humiliation burned themselves out and he returned to his usual, reasonable self. She thumbed into her voicemail and saw seven messages waiting for her. One by one, she listened to them. All from Mother. Angry, so angry. The words were barbs: "stupid", "crazy", "embarrassment". Then the last one.

"Where are you? I'm worried . . . " A soft hiccough, perhaps a sob. "Just let me know you're all right."

Sara put the phone back in the bottom drawer of the dresser.

After her fourth week at the hotel, Neville raised his eyebrows when she came down to pay for another week in advance.

"I thought you said you wouldn't be here very long," he said, filling out the form again and getting her to sign it.

"I'm as surprised as you are," she said. She'd expected to be in Asgard. All she'd had though were the little glimpses when her enemies were

91

defeated, tantalising glimpses into a world that roared with beauty. Instead of being there, she was stuck in urban limbo.

Her hands had healed quickly with no scars and no loss of movement. She twirled the pen once between her fingers before handing it back to him.

"Got a busload of tourists in today," he said. "I've put them on the third floor so they don't wake you up while you're sleeping, but sorry if there's noise."

"I appreciate that."

She crossed the reception area and pushed open the door, stepped out into the evening. Work wasn't for another few hours, and she had an urge for very strong coffee. She walked the three blocks to her favourite café, ordered a double espresso, and sat under a fluorescent light sipping it, looking out into the street.

She saw him then. She hadn't seen him for a long time and while she hadn't forgotten about him, she had dismissed him as unimportant. The blond man. She had come to think of him as the Viking, because of his appearance and because she spent a lot of time reading about Viking mythology on the internet these days. There he was—the Viking—standing across the street from the café, semi-hidden by a bus shelter.

He wasn't one of Odin's challenges and she knew this because she hadn't dreamed of runes. She had seen him too many times now for it to be a coincidence, surely. She watched him while she finished her coffee, and he watched her. Then she rose, walked to the door, and pushed it open.

The Viking saw her emerge. Traffic passed between them, stopping her from running across the road and demanding he explain why he was following her. He smiled at her and called out, in a thick European accent, "You will regret being born."

Her stomach went cold. "What do you mean?" she called back, but then a bus trundled along and by the time it had passed, he was gone.

Sara realised that if there was a Viking running around the City delivering strange prophecies, Benjamin Midnight, fascinated as he was with investigating the paranormal, might know something about it. He came in every Wednesday night to listen to the bands, but had not tried to make conversation with her again. She guessed this was because she'd all but accused him of stalking her. That Wednesday, when she approached him in the break between the band's sets, he looked more surprised than happy that she wanted to speak to him.

"Hi," she said.

"Hi," he answered warily.

"I'm sorry if I was rude to you," she ventured, straining her voice over the sounds of the crowd and the canned music.

"No, I was rude to you. I asked too many questions and I had no right to. I was overly . . . interested."

"I need to ask you about something, but now's not the time. Too noisy. How about that coffee?"

He nodded quickly. "Sure. When . . . ?"

"Seven tomorrow morning. The café on Duke Street with the lime green seats. Do you know it?"

"Yes, I do."

"You need to know this: if you blog about me or about our meeting or about anything I tell you, I will break all your fingers."

He smiled, then realised she might be serious. "You can trust me. I promise you."

"Good. Talk then."

Sara went back to her post by the door, surveying the room, aware of Ben's eyes on her from afar.

Spring rain washed the streets as she walked to meet him the next day. She had brushed the cigarette smoke out of her hair and put on a dress, now both were soaked. The door of the café swung open into dry warmth. He was already there, sitting at a table under a painting of two pink coffee cups, pretending to be very interested in his phone.

She slid into the seat opposite him. "Hi, thanks for meeting me," she said.

"You're sodden," he replied, slipping his phone into the satchel that hung on the back of his chair.

"I know."

"You need an umbrella."

"I guess you're right. I didn't think it would be this bad. I thought I could stay under awnings. But the rain's coming down hard."

The waitress brought over Ben's hot chocolate and took Sara's order.

"You don't drink coffee then?" she asked him as he shook a sugar packet and dumped its contents into the cup.

"Not often. It upsets my stomach." He stirred furiously, splashing some of the hot chocolate on the saucer. He didn't seem to notice. "I suppose you need the caffeine in your line of work. Doing the night shift."

"I'm tired all the time," she said. "But that's not just from working nights. I'm tired of the City and I'm tired of waiting."

"What are you waiting for?"

"Something." She smiled. "Isn't everyone though?"

"I suppose." He took a sip of his drink then sat back. "What did you want to ask me about?"

"I've seen a man, three times now. I think he's following me, or at least he's interested in me . . . I call him the Viking. He looks . . . well, like a Viking. Long blond hair, weird clothes. I saw him a few days ago and he called out something cryptic, almost prophetic, to me. I wondered if in your investigations you'd come across anything about him."

Ben shook his head. "No. Not familiar at all. What did he say to you?"

"He said, 'You will regret being born.'"

"And do you?"

"Do I what?"

"Regret being born?"

"Um . . . no. Not yet anyway. He was talking future tense, after all." She tried to laugh, to make light of it.

Ben seemed to be turning it over in his mind. Sara's coffee arrived and she sipped it slowly.

At length, he said, "Why did you think I might know something about your Viking?"

"Because of the *Midnight Post*. That's what you're interested in, right? Mysteries. Weird happenings."

"So you believe me? Because you know a lot of people think I'm a . . . crackpot."

Sara reflected on the things she'd learned, the things she'd seen, since

Odin had turned up at her house. "I don't think you're a crackpot. Beyond our ordinary lives, there are things past our imagining."

"Yes," he said, a fervent gleam lighting his eyes. "Yes, absolutely."

"But I don't believe in alien abductions," she said with a smile, leaning back in her chair. "I think you're all wrong on that one."

He laughed loudly, and it was a lovely sound. When he laughed, all his awkwardness seemed to evaporate.

"Listen," he said, "I have a lot of friends who tip me off. Do you want me to ask around about the Viking?"

"I suppose it can't hurt."

"Are you worried about it?"

She considered this for a moment. "I'm not worried he'll hurt me. I'm more than able to protect myself."

"Agreed," he said.

"It's more that I'm unsettled by him. Like there is something going on between me and him, and he's the only one who knows what it is." She shrugged, picked up her coffee cup again. "But maybe I'm wrong. Maybe he's just a general nutter, and not a nutter specifically interested in me."

"Plenty of nutters in the City," he said in agreement. Then added with a merry curl of his lip, "Many of them are my friends."

At that moment, his mobile phone began to ring. He drew his satchel into his lap and began rummaging in it, pulling out an array of contents: wallet, keys, notebooks, electrical doo-dads. Phone in hand, he said, "Excuse me, I have to take this," and turned his shoulder away.

Sara tried not to listen, but nonetheless she caught Ben's half of the conversation. "Hey, how's it going? . . . .Yep, I told you . . . .Have there been others? . . . .Corner of Prince and Duchess, yep . . . .We'll give it a week, and then maybe go down there . . . .I don't know, we'll take a torch or something . . . .Yep, okay. Bye." He hung up and turned back to Sara. "Sorry, investigating a case. Noises in the sewers."

"Giant crocodiles?"

"Hey, no teasing."

She indicated all his belongings on the table. "What is all this stuff?"

"Paranormal hunting kit," he said sheepishly, pointing to the objects one by one. "Thermal flashlight, EVP recorder, all-spectrum camcorder, EMF meter, laser grid scope . . . want me to go on?"

"And using this stuff, you can tell if there's a supernatural presence around?"

"Yes."

"Really?"

He set his jaw, the first time she'd seen him less than puppy-dog passive. "Yes. Really."

"So if I was . . . supernatural in some way, all this equipment would start blinking and ringing?"

Now he tilted his head slightly to the side, regarding her closely through his glasses. "Not necessarily. Also, are you trying to tell me something?"

She carefully placed her empty coffee cup on the table. "Maybe next time," she said. "I need to go home to bed."

"Can I call you?"

"I keep my phone switched off."

He rummaged in his satchel again, pulled out an old bus ticket and scribbled on the back of it. "Here's my number. In case you switch it back on."

She took it, turned it over between her fingers. It was a ticket to

Zone 2, the east side of the City, notorious for gang crime and prostitution.

"See you at the club then?" he asked.

"Yes, sure."

Back at the hotel, she stopped briefly at the computer and went back to Ben's blog. His last update was about strange noises coming from the storm drain on the corner of Prince Street and Duchess Street, about half a mile from where Sara was staying.

My source reports hearing a roaring sound, and a female voice shouting in a strange language. My source recorded this shouting and played it to a colleague who insists she is speaking some form of old Germanic.

Sara wasn't sure how much credit to give Ben's source. A lot of rain had fallen in the last week, and storm drains always flowed with white noise that could be interpreted mysteriously by those with big imaginations. But strange and dangerous things did exist in the world, and Sara knew that better than anybody.

Two days later, she dreamed of runes again, burning across her field of vision. This time, the dream came with pain. Long lines of gut-aching nerve pain drawing down from her head and into her stomach. When she woke, it took two minutes for the pain to abate. Then she rose and rummaged in her drawer for the print-out of the rune interpretation. *Modgudr.*

Sara pulled on clothes and drew up the blind. Rain fell heavily from leaden clouds.

Each time the runes had come, so had the monster. She knew now it was Odin's way of warning her what was coming, but she hadn't a clue what a Modgudr was and where it might be lurking. Still, her blood leapt at the thought. Third challenge. Four to go. Then the universe would open up for her, and she would be in a place and time beyond imagining with her kin. Her *real* kin. Not the Midgard kin who had taught her to be ashamed.

"You're on the internet all the time," Neville said, later, when she sat down to search for Modgudr. "You've got a social media addiction."

"Not on social media," she said as the list of search responses came up. "I don't need friends."

"Everybody needs friends." Then he was busy with a couple who came in off the street, soaked and trawling suitcases behind them.

This time, the search had thrown up useful information. Modgudr, it seemed, was a giantess who guarded a bridge over a river in the underworld realm of Hel. Sara clicked through to an old medieval story that Modgudr featured in.

Hermod rode nine nights through deep and dark valleys, and did not see light until he came to the Gjöll and rode across the Gjallarbru, which shines with gold. Modgudr is the name of the old portress who guarded the bridge. She asked him for his name, and of what kin he was . . .

This last detail struck her as familiar, and she remembered the *Midnight Post's* report. A woman's voice shouting in a foreign language. Underworld. River. The drains under the City running with storm water.

But if Modgudr was here in the City, why hadn't she come looking for Sara? Just how big was a giantess? Too big to fit through the opening to a storm drain?

Like will find like.

Maybe it was Sara's turn to hunt one down.

After work, she didn't take the familiar route home to the hotel. Instead, she headed a little further south towards the river. The rain hadn't let up. The gutters were swollen and Sara was soaked in minutes. She didn't mind. She expected she would get wetter yet.

In her left hand, she gripped the waterproof torch she had borrowed from Ally's store room. Her right hand was deep in her pocket. In time, she found herself at the intersection between Prince Street and Duchess Street, standing on the heavy iron grate over the storm drain. Water poured down it. She listened for a while, but couldn't hear anything. She crouched on the grate, shining her torch into it. The torchbeam picked up a set of iron sleepers embedded into the wall for access.

A loud car horn behind her made her jolt and drop the torch. A car full of late night revellers shouted something obscene out to her then sped off into the night. Her fury at them surprised her. She wanted to run after them and grab their car and turn it upside down and shake them all out onto the cold, hard bitumen. But they were long gone now. The streets were empty.

Sara put her hands in the centre of the grate and pulled. Cement and iron gave way from each other. She placed the grate up on the footpath, crouched at the edge of the hole she had made, and took the first step onto the iron ladder. She tucked the torch into her waistband and made her way down, then stepped off the ladder. The stormwater was nearly a foot deep. Sara switched on the torch again and shone it from side to side. A massive pipe, at least eight feet high and as wide as her hotel room, led away into the darkness. Which direction?

She decided to follow the direction of the water, to the south.

The rain water was cold around her calves and she shivered as she sloshed through it. The smell of clean water laid over something more ancient: mud and limestone. She swept her torchbeam in front of her. Debris bobbed on the stream: bottle caps and cigarette butts and plastic packaging. It bumped into her legs softly as she went, then was dragged by the force of the water away and ahead of her. The walls rumbled and she realised she must be near a train station. She waited for the noise to pass, then sloshed forward again. The pipe took a bend, and she rounded it warily, shone her torchbeam. Nothing.

Ben's source had heard voices from the storm drain back at Prince and Duchess. Sara didn't want to go too much further in the wrong direction, so she turned and began to retrace her steps, trudging against the flow this time, her big thigh muscles aching from the effort. She saw the open culvert overhead. Wind whipped down it and ran past her as she kept moving into the dark.

No, not quite as dark as she'd thought. Something softly gleaming ahead, picking up the edge of her torch beam.

And then the noise. The horrific, tearing roar of a beast. It shook Sara's nerves loose and she stopped.

Her torch light extinguished. She was plunged into darkness.

There she stood, water flowing around her calves, eyes open and unseeing. She could hear her own pulse and her own ragged breathing. Modgudr, like Odin, was powerful enough to interfere with electrical currents. Sara knew that if she simply stood still, the light would flicker back on in just a few minutes. But to wait there in the dark, not knowing how close the monster was in the roaring darkness, loosened her guts.

Time stretched out. What if her torch didn't come back on? Her eyes had adjusted now and she could barely make out anything. Blue phosphorescence in the water that was so pale it might be imagined. A smoky blur where the ceiling might be. The monster had gone quiet. Sara listened hard.

Then the torch flared into life, and Modgudr was standing in front of her, two armspans away.

She was nearly as tall as the ceiling of the drain. Her hair was long and dark, hanging in lank curls to her hulking shoulders. Modgudr was huge in every sense: a mountain of flesh. Rolling with fat, cheeks wide and dense with bone, mouth roaring and stretched, teeth like piano keys, protuberant eyeballs as big and glassy as snowglobes, and hands like bunches of bananas. She saw Sara and put one foot forward, thundering onto the ground and sending a shudder along the pipe.

Modgudr took an enormous breath and bellowed a sentence at Sara. Although she didn't understand the language, Sara knew what the old giantess had said.

"My name is Sara," Sara shouted back at her. "I am Odin's daughter."

Modgudr drew enormous breath again, making the wind swirl in the tunnel. Then she roared, arms spread wide.

She was big. But she was slow. Sara waited. Modgudr lashed out with a meaty arm, knocking Sara's torch so it flew up and cracked the ceiling, then landed with a splash in the water. Its beam shone directly up, through the river, lending only a glimmer of waterlogged light to the scene. Sara could see her opponent well enough: she was too big to miss.

102

Sara grasped Modgudr's arm and pulled on it hard, but Modgudr pulled it back just as hard and Sara nearly lost her footing. Modgudr took advantage of this, walloping Sara on the shoulder wildly. Sara cried out in pain and shock.

This was going to be harder than she'd anticipated.

Sara staggered back a few steps. Modgudr raised her fist again and this time Sara caught it, twisted with all her might and flung Modgudr against the wall. Chips of cement flew. The giant stood back and shook her head roughly, as if to clear it. Sara took the opportunity to plough into her with her shoulder, pushing her against the wall again. Then, half-climbing on her opponent's back, she fisted the giant's hair and used it to slam her head against the wall repeatedly.

Modgudr twisted and shook, but Sara clung tight. So the giant spread her arms wide, and simply fell backwards. Onto Sara.

Sara's mouth and nose were filled with the stale, mouldy smell of the giant's hair for a moment, and then she was in the water. It ran cold and airless across her face, and breath wouldn't come. She struggled, couldn't find which way was up and which down, but grasped two handful's of Modgudr's flesh and twisted and pushed until the giant moved just enough for her to get leverage to pull her face out of the water. Crooking her arm around Modgudr's neck she managed to get her body half-out from under, choking her opponent in the process. Modgudr lashed out with fists that hit the water like rocks, but Sara used all her might to flip the giant off her and over. Modgudr was now face down in the gushing storm water, and Sara sat on the back of her head, landing hard punches on her skull.

Modgudr struggled but Sara held firm.

The vision shimmered over her senses, and she saw she stood on a great wide bridge in a fathomless cavern. The bridge was made of some opalescent stone that gleamed dully in the light of flaming torches in elaborate gold brackets. Below the bridge ran a swirling river, icy and black. Its dark, glittering beauty made Sara catch her breath.

Splash! Sara collapsed into the storm water. Modgudr was gone, winked out of existence like the others.

She sat up slowly, coughing and spitting water and hair out of her mouth, waist-deep in the river. The vision had skidded past her fingertips now, but she wanted to pull it back towards her and inhabit it again. She understood now that the vision was the underworld bridge where Modgudr lived, that all of the visions came from the minds of her opponents. That's why they seemed familiar, like an arrival home, every time she experienced one. These were glimpses of Asgard, the world that soon she would step into, and it seemed so much more deep and broad and high than the flat world she knew, that she almost couldn't bear to climb to her feet and take her saturated body back up on to the ordinary streets of the City.

The rain stayed for days, but then cleared to blue spring weather. The City seemed to stay wintry, the bleak cold trapped between skyscrapers. Sara went to sleep every morning hoping to dream of runes. Three of seven monsters down. She wasn't even halfway to Asgard, and she needed to get there soon, before her nerve failed her.

She dreamed about Mother one late afternoon. Sara was still a child in the dream, and Mother was tying her shoelaces for her.

"I don't want you to trip," she said, but Sara realised Mother was tying her shoelaces together.

"I won't be able to walk if you do that."

"Better that you can't walk than that you trip. You might get hurt."

Sara woke then, to the sound of the garbage truck emptying the recycling bin behind the hotel. The clatter and smash of glass falling. She missed her mother. A deep ache had pierced her guts. Memories washed through her, sweet and sore as bruises.

It wouldn't hurt to go see her. To talk to her and explain. Here she was, unafraid of giants and witches, but afraid of her mother's anger and sorrow.

Before she could change her mind, Sara was up and dressed, slinging her bag over her shoulder and making her way to the interchange.

She reached her mother's house just on dusk, and almost lost her nerve when she saw it by daylight. This ordinary place where she'd spent so much of her childhood. She stood opposite, stomach churning. Then gathered her resolve and crossed the road, knocked hard on the door.

The last thing she was prepared for was no answer. She knocked again, but already she could hear the hollowness in her knocks and then she remembered: Mother and Pete had an overseas holiday booked. At the time Mother had told her about it, she'd been little concerned with it, so consumed was she with wedding preparation. But now she did the calculations in her head, she knew she'd come to an empty house. One that would be empty for at least another two weeks.

Sara rested her hand lightly on the door and stood there for a long time, glutting on the melancholy feeling of being home but not home, here but not here. Time had passed. Things had changed. Overhead, birds arrowed by in flocks, heading to their nests for the evening.

Sara left her mother's house as dusk gathered around her, walked down to the bus stop and sat to wait. Traffic surged past. Headlights and streetlights alike came on. She leaned her head back on the perspex and closed her eyes, just for a moment.

She became aware somebody was standing in front of her.

Sara's eyes flicked open. It was the Viking. He caught her in his gaze.

"Who are you?" she said, unconsciously shrinking away from him on the seat.

"You and I," he said slowly, almost guttural, "we are linked."

"I have no idea who you are. What's your name? Are you one of Odin's creatures?"

He laughed and shook his head. "Odin does not own me," he spat. "I am not of his blood or making."

"Then how are we linked?"

"Blood feud," he said.

"What does that even mean?"

He saw a group of people approaching and began to walk away.

"Wait!" She leapt up from her seat and reached for him, and he began to run. Darting between traffic, which beeped and shouted at him. She followed, made it to the traffic island and lurched forward to cross the rest of the way. Truck brakes screeched and she wheeled back, couldn't go after him without getting squashed.

When the truck had passed and she could see her way across the busy street, it was too late. He was nowhere in sight.

We are linked.

But how could they be? She knew nothing about him. Yet somehow, she had always known they were linked. That was why his appearance unsettled her so. Something about her blood recognised his.

Blood feud. She had no idea what the term meant, but it didn't sound like a happy occasion. Across the street, her bus back to the City came and went.

Sara started walking.

III BLOOD FEUD

"She was hardy at fighting, wherever she aimed her blows."

—*Greenlandic Poem of Atli*

CHAPTER ONE

HEL'S WATCHDOG

*B*LOOD FEUD. BLOOD FEUD. SARA KEPT the phrase in her head, afraid she would forget it before she had a chance to research what it meant. *Blood feud.* It kept time with her footsteps back from the interchange, and when she burst into the foyer of the dim hotel where she was staying, she had burned the phrase into her mind.

She booted up the internet computer. It made a sick noise then blinked at her once.

"It's dead," Neville proclaimed from behind the counter.

"Can I borrow a pen?"

He held it out for her and she took it, wrote the words *blood feud* on her hand.

Neville peered over the counter. "What does that mean?"

"I don't know yet. But my memory's not all that great." She handed him his pen. Was there time to get to the library across town and back before work tonight? Then she remembered it was Wednesday. Ben would be at the club. He might be able to help her unpack the mystery. Why was she linked to the Viking?

Ben wasn't at the club. She fought down her disappointment and got on with her evening. It was a busy one, with three separate fights to break up and a chance to evict a shrill-voiced young woman who had drunk too much and decided to stand next to Sara and call her a "fucking fat bitch". Throwing human bodies out of the club was arousing dangerous feelings, the kind of frustrated smoulder that had been her constant companion for all the years before she met her father. She had to be careful to pull all her punches, and she didn't want to be careful anymore. She wanted to be in Asgard, where she could be free.

Patience, Sara. Patience.

Back in her hotel room after work, she switched on her phone. It sat dead in her hand for a moment, and she was reaching for the charger when it surged into life with an apologetic beep. She found the scrap of paper with Ben's number on it, and dialled it. It rang out, and she remembered it was three-thirty in the morning. He'd be sleeping. She had become so nocturnal she'd forgotten other people slept at night, not during the day.

Sara was halfway out of her boots when her phone rang. She picked it up curiously. The number was familiar: she had just dialled it.

"Ben?" she said.

"Sara? You switched your phone on."

"Yes, I did. I did."

"You woke me up."

"I forgot it was so late."

"What's wrong?"

"You weren't at the club."

"I've been working on an investigation. Had to go on a stake-out." He chuckled at himself. "You didn't answer. What's wrong?"

"I think I need your help."

"Come over."

"Now?"

"Why not?"

He gave her an address in Zone 2, then said, "Keep your phone switched on. That way I can find you if I need to."

"So can . . . other people. From my past." Even as she said this, she realised no angry messages from Dillon or her mother had downloaded. They had stopped trying to find her.

"Don't be afraid. Especially not of the past."

She smiled, even though she knew he couldn't see her. "I'll be there really soon."

Trains ran between the City and Zone 2 twenty-four hours a day. Sara walked down to the interchange and through the echoing concourse. A machine scanned her ticket. The security camera above her whirred, but she was the only soul there. On the platform, she sat on one of the long aluminium benches bolted to the wall and waited. A fluorescent light above her head flickered. A man in a brown hoodie sat further down the platform, muttering and nodding into his chest. His feet were bare and Sara winced at the thought of how cold they must be, even in this milder weather. The approaching train echoed in the tunnel, a cold gust ahead of it. Sara stood, waited for the door to open, then took a seat inside. As they slid away, the door to the next carriage clattered open and the man in the brown hoodie came in. He stood in the aisle, swaying slightly, considering Sara through bloodshot eyes.

She bristled, squared up her shoulders, ready to fight.

"You're one of them," he said.

"One of what?"

"I can smell 'em. You're one." He wrinkled his nose as though it was she who was filling the carriage with a malodorous stench, and not him. He grabbed the back of the seat in front of her and leaned in. "You come from somewhere else. Somewhere unholy."

Sara recoiled from him and he straightened and strode down to the end of the carriage. Was he just raving, or could he actually tell whether somebody was a person or a monster? And was she becoming a monster? *One of them?* She looked behind her. His gaze was fixed on her, his fingers hard over a cross on a string around his neck. She climbed to her feet and slowly made her way down the aisle to him, stopped beside him. Her pulse flicked at her throat. Spoiling for a fight.

"You know nothing about me," she whispered, close to his ear, nostrils filled with the sour smell of his hair.

"I know enough. I've seen things." He sneered at her. "I know a devil when I see one."

Her hand shot out, almost without thought, and closed around his neck. She half-lifted him out of his seat. His hands flailed. "I'm not a devil," she spat. "I'm Odin's daughter." Then she released him and he shot to his feet and ran away into the next carriage.

114

Sara stalked back to her seat, thudding heart slowing. She couldn't do things like that. She'd get herself in trouble. Arrested. In the watch-house with no chance to meet Odin's remaining challenges. She looked at her hands, which had seconds ago held a man's life in the balance. They appeared to be ordinary women's hands: soft and white, with nails cut short. Not the hands of a killer. A devil.

The train pulled in to Zone 2 station and Sara climbed off. She didn't expect to hear her name called. She turned towards the voice. "Ben?"

The platform was empty, deep underground. The smell of diesel freight trains that had been through seemed to have permeated the rock and stone. Ben stood among the iron and steel and he looked very mortal: skinny, pale, his hair curling over his collar in an almost feminine way. Sara felt a pang for his vulnerability and wondered if she should walk away, leave him be. Monsters chased her.

He fell into step alongside her. "I walked down here to meet you. My place is hard to find. Come on."

Ben led her up the long escalator and onto a street that ran along the train line, then zigzagged through the alleyways behind China Town. He stopped at a lime green door behind a restaurant and opened it with a key. "Up here," he said.

She looked up. The building was a brown brick block, completely unremarkable. "People live here?"

"A few of us." He closed the door behind him and hit the security light in the stairwell. "It's an old office block and the demolition orders are in process. Cheapest rent you can imagine. One more flight of stairs."

The security light flicked out and they took the last flight in the

115

dark. He opened the door and she found herself standing inside a square room. A corner was given over to a kitchenette. A mattress lay on the floor. The only other furniture was a desk under a painted window. No natural light. A mouldy smell.

"It's not grand, I know," he said apologetically.

She shrugged. "I'm living in a hotel. I can't criticise."

He pulled out the chair behind his desk and offered it to her. "Please, sit down. You want a cup of coffee?"

"Yeah, thanks. Strong and sweet please."

He laughed. "I think that's where I'm supposed to say, 'like you.'"

"Resist the urge," she replied. "So what's the stake-out?"

His eyes lit up. "A massive grey dog. I've had three separate reports about it. I'm getting my investigation together, but it looks like it might have made a home in the scrap metal lot on the north side of the City. I'm heading out there later today to see if I can get some photos." Then he checked himself. "Sorry. I know I sound like a geek."

"Don't apologise. That's kind of why I'm here. Because you're a geek and you know things."

"I don't know much at all."

"Do you know what a blood feud is?"

He filled the kettle in his sink. "No idea. Go ahead and google it."

She pulled the chair up at the computer, pushing aside books and papers. Volumes on wolf behaviour. Print-outs of emails. A copy of *Hound of the Baskervilles*. A map of the City with red crosses marked on it. While he made her instant coffee, she searched the internet for information on blood feuds.

"Well?" he said, handing her a cup a few minutes later.

She read it out aloud to him. "In early Germanic societies, a system

116

by which a score is settled among families or tribes. A continuous quarrel that can be passed between generations. Murderous hostilities in the name of debts and reparation."

"And who are you in a blood feud with?"

"A Viking." She explained to him about her encounter, aware that her voice was becoming breathless as she went on.

He perched on the edge of his desk. "But why are you worried? I've seen you carry drunks out of the bar. Surely he's not much threat to you."

"I get this feeling when he's near me," she said. "A kind of . . . primitive fear. I know that sounds crazy."

"Nothing sounds crazy to me." He indicated the collection of research on his desk.

"If I just knew who he was," she said. "Then I might have an idea what my debt to him is. And what he intends to do about it." Because he'd had ample opportunity to try to kill her if that was what he wanted to do. He'd been following her movements for weeks. She'd had her eyes closed at the bus stop when he had sat right next to her. But he'd mostly chosen to stay hidden or to run.

Ben sipped his coffee thoughtfully, then said, "I know somebody who can help."

"You do?"

"One of my . . . contacts. Cyrena. She's a psychic."

Sara blinked back any disbelief. The things she'd seen in the past weeks meant there was no room for scepticism any more. "Can you arrange for her to see me?"

117

Cyrena plied her trade from a top floor flat in a high-rise. Her apartment building was on a long hilly street that caught the wind. Sara shivered as Ben pressed the security buzzer and waited. In the bottom of the building was a café, closed and dark with chairs up on tables. They waited a few minutes then Ben buzzed again.

"It's really early," Sara said. "We'll wake her up."

"She won't mind."

Finally, a crackly voice said, "Yes?"

"Aunty Cyrena, it's Ben."

"Come on up." The door buzzed open and they stepped in out of the wind.

"Aunty Cyrena?" Sara asked.

"Yeah. Not a real Aunty. But she was my next-door neighbour growing up." He pressed the button on the lift. "I used to go to her place after school, before my mum was home from work. Then she moved here and I didn't see her for years."

"Did you track her down?"

"We found each other. Through my work. She was . . . changed."

"What do you mean?"

The lift arrived, smelling of piss and bleach.

"I'll tell you later," Ben said.

A few moments later, Cyrena was letting them into her apartment, a colour-burst of space whose walls were pinned with postcards from mystical places: Glastonbury Tor, Stonehenge, Easter Island, the Pyramids, Machu Picchu. Cyrena herself looked remarkably normal: a middle-aged woman with dyed red hair, silver roots peeking out, whose body showed she'd enjoyed her food and wine her whole life.

She was wearing a wine-coloured silk dressing gown that was stained and threadbare.

"Come in, Ben, my darling. And look, you've brought a friend." Cyrena smiled at Sara, then her smile froze a moment and her eyes flickered. "Oh," she said.

"Aunty Cyrena, this is Sara. She needs your help."

"Yes, she certainly does." Cyrena ran a hand through her hair. "Just give me a moment to get dressed. I must look a fright."

She disappeared down the corridor and Ben and Sara sat on a soft red couch.

"Has she ever told your future?" Sara asked Ben.

He shook his head. "She wasn't always a psychic. She used to be a high school maths teacher." He dropped his voice low. "Then she developed a brain tumour, inoperable. Since then, she's had pyschic visions. We help each other find things, and share information."

"Wow."

"Yeah. And she's very good. Forget what other psychics have told you; her insights are spot on."

"I've never been to a psychic," Sara said. Once, in high school, Sara had been invited (grudgingly) to a sleepover party with all of the other girls in her class. When Mother found out there would be a fortune teller there, she had forbidden her to go. "It's a load of nonsense and superstition and it will put ideas in your head," Mother had said. Now, on reflection, she wondered if her mother harboured concerns that a psychic would tell her something about her secret strength, her true lineage, her father.

"Now," Cyrena said, bustling back into the room in a grey tracksuit.

"Let's look at you properly, Sara." Cyrena grasped Sara's hand and pulled her to her feet, looking her up and down. "My word," she said. "What on earth are you?"

"What do you . . . ?" Ben started.

"I don't even know," Sara answered. "But I'm becoming something."

"You certainly are."

"What are you two talking about?" Ben asked.

"I'll explain next time," Sara said to him.

"I think you've made that promise before."

"Privacy, Ben," Cyrena said, shooing him off. "Go watch TV in my bedroom. Sara, sit."

So Sara sat while Ben grudgingly slunk off.

Cyrena sat next to her and held out her hands, palms up. "Lay your hands on mine," she said.

"I don't want a reading," Sara said, resting her hands across Cyrena's cool palms. "I have a specific question to ask."

"I can't figure you out," Cyrena said, as though she hadn't heard. "Half from here and half from . . . where?"

"Asgard," Sara said. "Though I've never been there."

Cyrena's eyebrows shot up. "Oh, my. I've never . . . " Her eyes grew misty. "Bless Ben for bringing you into my life. You glow, my dear. How beautiful to feel that glow, even once."

Sara met her gaze. "A man on the train said I was a devil."

"People are afraid of what they don't understand."

"I'm afraid of myself sometimes. Should I be?"

Cyrena didn't answer straight away. She seemed to be choosing her words carefully when she said, "You are not a great intellect."

"I know that."

"Immense physical power not tempered by thought . . . yes, that is dangerous." She smiled. "Or it can be. Still, you didn't come for amateur philosophy, did you? What do you need to know?"

Sara pressed her palms harder into Cyrena's. The older woman's hands were very soft, like butter. "A man has been following me," she said. "He says we are linked somehow. But how? It's vital I know."

Cyrena inhaled deeply, dropped her head and closed her eyes. Sara could see her eyeballs moving left to right under her lids, almost as though she were dreaming. But Cyrena was still awake.

"The blond man in the dark clothes?" she asked.

"Yes. You're good."

The corner of Cyrena's mouth lifted in a smile. "I'm trying my hardest to impress you."

"I'm nobody important to impress," Sara muttered. "Who is he?"

Cyrena's forehead creased in concentration. A minute passed. Another. Then Cyrena withdrew her hands, sat up straight, and opened her eyes.

"He's your brother," she said.

My brother. Sara hardly heard the questions Ben fired at her rapidly as they walked back downtown towards her hotel in the gritty morning light. "What did she say?" "What did she mean by 'what are you'?" "Did she know who he was?" "Did she say anything else about you?"

Finally, Sara turned to him and said sharply, "Ben, stop!"

He stopped talking, but also stopped walking, expression like a kicked puppy. She could see the traffic light behind her change green in the reflection in his glasses.

"I'm not one of your freaks," she said. "I'm not . . . something to investigate and blog about."

"I'm sorry," he said. "I didn't mean . . . " He put both his hands up. "I'll leave you be."

He turned, and she watched him go, and she was glad. She was only here temporarily.

As always, she repressed the other option: that somehow she would fail and not be able to join her father in Asgard. Presumably if she couldn't defeat one of her opponents, that would mean she wouldn't be alive to regret it.

Sara went back to her hotel room and climbed back into bed.

My brother. How was it possible? She knew Mother had no other children, and the Viking had said himself that Odin bore no relation to him. *I am not of his blood or making.* His words played over in her head as she tried to sleep.

It took her nearly an hour, but finally she worked it out. Mother had no other children. He wasn't Odin's son. But there was somebody else, wasn't there? The woman Odin had impregnated, the "young mortal woman". He'd said that he sent Sara into the future, but what had that really meant? Had the woman survived it? Did she have a young son that she left behind? Sara's skin prickled lightly. And if that was the case, how had he found his way a thousand years into the future?

Sara turned these questions over as she pushed herself hopelessly against the wall of sleep, while the spring day warmed outside.

Somehow, she fell into a doze. She woke to an afternoon thunderstorm, cracking over the skyscrapers and echoing down into the streets and alleys. Runes were burning in her mind's eye. She quickly wrote them down, consulted her guide.

GARMR

Her next challenge was on its way, and here she was, weary and unable to focus. The rain hammered against her window and she curled up and tried to go back to sleep, but it retreated even further from her; her head split with a headache that made all her nerves contract.

Tired and in pain, she knew she had to find out who Garmr was.

Sara rose and dressed. Her stomach rumbled angrily. Outside, the rain still fell heavily, and she waited under the awning of the hotel a few minutes for it to ease, dazed and dreading the day. On the walk to the public library, she stopped for a flapjack and a strong coffee. Then, devouring her very late breakfast, she walked up to the top of King Street and climbed the wide stone stairs, passed between the doric columns and into the library. The black-and-white chequered floor was traced with lines of water from dripping umbrellas, and she nearly slipped on her way to the reading room. She consulted the catalogue and wrote her book order on the slip to hand to the soft-handed young woman behind the counter.

"It will take about ten minutes," she said. "You can't have any food or drink in the reading room." She indicated Sara's coffee cup.

"Sorry," Sara said, tipping the contents into her mouth quickly. "There. All gone."

The girl pulled her mouth into a disapproving line, and Sara went to sit and wait by one of the white oval tables where studious people read and took notes.

It took less than two minutes for the girl to return and call out her name. Sara took the book—*Myths of the Vikings*—and opened up to the index while still standing at the counter.

"You can sit down if you like," the girl said.

"No need," Sara muttered, skimming the entry quickly. *The giant dog who guards the entrance to Helheim (Hel's home), which is the realm of the dead.*

A dog. Odin had sent her a dog to fight.

And Sara knew exactly where she would find him.

The rain eased and the clouds cleared away to reveal a dusk-darkening sky on her walk from the bus stop to the scrap-metal lot. Her weariness evaporated too, as the desire in her blood awoke, surging and bubbling in her veins. She felt her hands, her muscles, her bones filling with wild, white-hot energy. The rain-damp streets smelled of earth and copper. She was on the outskirts of the City now, walking past chain-link fences and huge industrial warehouses. The traffic was sparser but louder, mostly made up of trucks and diesel tradesmen's vans. She approached the edge of the deserted scrap-metal lot and saw that it stretched out for nearly half a mile down the road. The fence was too high to climb and if she had climbed it, it was topped with three rows of razor wire. Sara stopped, looked around. Waited for the traffic to pass. Then ripped a hole in the chain link and walked straight in.

After the heavy rain, the packed dirt floor of the lot had turned into a mud bath. Tidy hills of gleaming junk stretched off into the distance. A yellow crane sat dormant between the far fence and a row of rusted skips, its claw resting on the ground. Crumpled cars were lined up against the fences. Sara started across the lot, picking her way around puddles. A shift from afternoon to evening, too subtle for Sara's eye to distinguish, set off the automatic security lights and they blazed into life and stared her down fiercely. The effect of the light— soft blue-pink twilight blended with harsh white spotlights—was to render the whole scene surreal. And to create shadows for monsters to hide in.

She kept walking, all her senses on alert for the approach of the dog. The last thing she expected was to hear somebody calling her name.

"Sara?"

Not a talking dog. Ben. Around his neck was a camera and in his hand he held a grey box that blinked when it pointed at her.

"Ben."

"What are you doing here?"

"The same as you, I think. Looking for a really big dog."

"What? Why?" He glanced down at the grey box. "Holy shit, this thing is going mental." He looked up again. "*You're* sending it mental."

Sara opened her mouth to respond, but at precisely the same moment the long, low howl of a dog issued from deep within the scrap-metal lot. She put her back to Ben and started towards it.

"Hey, wait for me," he said.

"You should go, Ben," she said. "I'll come see you after. I'll tell you everything. But it's not safe for you to be here."

"Are you serious? I've been tracking this dog for nearly a week. I want to see it."

"It's more dangerous than you can imagine," she said. "And I don't have time to explain."

She heard his footsteps stop, and presumed he'd heeded her warning.

She moved in between the hills of junk, ears strained for sounds that would betray Garmr's whereabouts. But there were no more howls. The sound of the crickets waking, trucks rumbling by on the distant highway, the crackle of a plastic bag caught by the wind in the tall chainlink fence. She negotiated her way between puddles and mud slicks, deeper and deeper into the lot.

Then she saw it: an immense black shape on top of one of the junk hills. A wolf the size of a horse, with fierce gold eyes that gleamed in the half-light. At her approach, it lifted its head and sniffed the twilight air, then slowly began to slink down the junk pile. Sara waited at the bottom, her heart swelling with strength.

But then there was a bright-white flash of light, and the beast stopped in its tracks. Sara half-turned to see where the light came from, and was surprised to see Ben with a camera.

"Sorry," he said, at the same time as she said, "Oh, no."

Garmr ran, brutally swift, directly for Ben. Thundering down the hill, hub caps and old saucepans and mattress springs and industrial scraps thrown up by his heels, the beast leapt and barrelled towards Ben. Sara blurred into action, jumped into the space between Garmr and Ben. The beast slammed with its full weight into her body, knocking all the air from her lungs and sending her flying into another junk hill. Something metal smacked down on her head, and she browned out for a few moments. She blinked rapidly, saw the dog approaching, sniffing, growling deep in its chest. Sara reached behind her, and her hand closed over something heavy and cool. She hefted it over her head, had time to register that it was the door of an industrial-sized oven, before she smashed it into Garmr's muzzle. The dog howled, and Sara climbed to her feet, looking around for Ben. She could see him lying, a dark figure on the muddy ground, a hundred yards away. The camera lay beside him.

"Ben!" she called, starting to run towards him, but then Garmr leapt again, a savage snarl filling her ears and a hot animal smell her nostrils. She twisted, drew back her arm and delivered a thudding punch to the beast's throat. Garmr took her down, lying half on top of her as he coughed and spat. She hooked her arm around his head and flipped him off her, then sat across the dome of his skull and rained punches down on his muzzle and eyes. The beast tried to snap at her, so she grasped his bottom jaw with one hand and his top jaw with the other and prised them apart until she felt sinew and bone snap.

And she stood at the gates of Hel. Vast, towering columns carved in obsidian with snakes and dragons and claw-footed lizards. Faraway sunlight, vertical shadows, waving grass as high as her hips undulating to the shushing of the wind—

The white flash went off again. At the same moment, Garmr disappeared from beneath her.

No! Not yet! It was over too quick, and her body was surging with white-hot energy. She couldn't pull it back; it would break her to pieces. She put her shoulder down and barrelled as fast as she could towards the wreck of a car. The blow sent it skidding sideways twenty feet. She leapt on top of the car and slammed her knuckles into the roof over and over again, until a valley formed in the metal and the surge in her body subsided.

Then she climbed down, strode towards Ben, who was staring at her open-mouthed. With blood-soaked hands she snatched the camera from his grasp, squeezed it with the last of the rage she felt in her blood, and the camera turned to dust.

"Hey!" he protested.

"You deserved that," she muttered.

He looked from her muddy face to the atomised camera in her hands, and said, "Yeah, I probably did."

CHAPTER TWO

NIGHTMARES

BACK AT HER HOTEL, SHE INSPECTED the wound on Ben's leg. A piece of flying metal had sliced through his jeans and carved a crooked smile on his left calf. She cleaned it for him and bandaged it with a scarf.

"How about you?" he said.

"I'm fine." She glanced at her knuckles, which were raw and bloody.

"I don't know how you're fine."

"I heal quickly." She slid her hands behind her back. "Anyway, I have to be at work in a few hours."

"Call in sick. Please. Call in sick and just sit here with me and . . . tell me everything. I want to know. What . . . What is it like to be you?"

Sara considered this question. She owed him nothing. Life would be so much easier if she didn't make any connections. She had already walked away from her two most significant connections: people who were twisted deep inside her soul. But neither Dillon nor Mother had ever pleaded to know what life was like for her. Her true, embodied experience of being here in Midgard had always been hidden or repressed out of necessity, for fear they wouldn't love her anymore. His simple question honoured her in a way those other, more intimate relationships never had. "Okay," she said.

She called Ally and excused herself from work with a headache, which wasn't entirely a lie. In fact, it was her whole body that ached from being pancaked under a giant wolf, but she wasn't about to tell that to her boss. Sara sat on the bed while Ben sat on the chair opposite her, waiting for her story. Night had fallen by now, and she switched on the yellow lamp to send the grey shadows back into their corners.

"Let me ask you something first," she said. "What did that grey box measure? The one you were pointing at me when I first found you at the scrap-metal lot."

"Electro-magnetic fields," he said. "Electro-magnetic energy is everywhere, of course, but the meter measures spikes."

"And what causes these spikes?"

"Broken microwaves can," he laughed. "But I use it to find paranormal entities."

"Paranormal? Do you think I'm a . . . monster?" Was she?

"I don't know what . . . who you are, Sara," he said. "I can't say I'm not curious, but I don't care, okay? I know you're a good person."

"I'm not a good person," she said. "If you think I'm some kind of saint, you've got that completely wrong."

"Then tell me about you. Tell me about the wolf."

"And the giant in the sewer."

"Giant? You knew about the thing in the drain as well?"

She laughed. "I'd say, 'you won't believe it', but I think you probably will."

Sara told him. She unfolded her whole story, her history and her heritage, her choice and her challenge. As the City sky bent towards midnight, she told her tale by the yellow light of the lamp in the grey room, her voice winding around her and around Ben, and drawing them into a loose knot that hadn't existed before. Ben sat very still and listened, occasionally asking her to elaborate or telling her not to rush or gloss over anything. Neither fear nor revulsion clouded his expression. If anything, his eyes took on an enraptured gleam and his whole body seemed to flex towards hers with happy excitement. When she was finished, he sprang from his chair.

"This is amazing. This is *amazing*!" He paced the small hotel room, between dresser and desk, passing her sitting on the bed over and over. "I knew it. I knew there was more than I could see and hear. I've always felt it. So you have three challenges to go?"

"Yes," she said. "And provided I defeat all of them . . . "

"Will you? Are they getting harder?"

She thought about how easily Garmr had been subdued, how she'd nearly filled her lungs with stormwater underneath Modgudr. "No. They're all different. There's no pattern. But I'm getting stronger."

"Of course you are." He stopped and gathered his satchel from the desk, pulling out his EMF meter. "The first night I met you, at the Club. You hauled that guy out under one arm as though he was a kindergardener. I'd never seen anything like it so I switched this on afterwards. It barely moved. Now look at it." He pointed the grey box at her, and she could see all the lights in the array were lit up and flashing wildly. "You're not just getting stronger. You're becoming more like them."

A swell of pride.

"You're going to Asgard," he said, breathless, shaking his head. Then he snapped his gaze up. "Take me with you?"

"I can't. At least, I don't think I can. I can't come back here to visit either. Odin says time passes differently."

"Odin, your dad," Ben said, smiling broadly.

Sara started laughing. "Yeah. Odin. My dad."

Ben went out for a bottle of wine from the liquor store and they filled the hotel tea-cups with it and drank it while watching a 1980s action movie on the television. Sara was comforted by the ordinariness of the situation, and happy to have company. It grew late or early, and she pulled the blind and said he could stay but not for sex. Just for comfort. Fully clothed, they curled up under the brown blankets and went to sleep.

The runes were under her eyelids almost immediately. She woke, seeing their imprint against the dark in the room just as if she had looked for too long at a lightbulb. She didn't need the sheet of paper; she knew them well enough now.

MARA

Mara was coming, sometime in the next twenty-four hours if experience held true. "Ben," she whispered into the dark. "I dreamed the runes again."

132

He stirred, made a little "mmm" sound, but didn't wake.

She put her head against his chest, breathing in his warmth and humanness. "Never mind," she said, and let herself slide back into sleep.

The curtains fan apart and a dark shape is revealed by the moon, full and close. A woman in a rocking chair. Sara approaches, compelled by a dreaming logic she does not understand. The woman turns her face and Sara recoils. She is at least a hundred years old, with fallen cheeks and small round eyes that glitter bird-like under hooded brows.

"Yes, come," she hisses, reaching out her fingers to caress Sara's cheek. As she does, horrible feelings rock through Sara's body. Anger and grief and despair. The hag smiles. Her teeth are tiny and brown. "Come and collect your nightmares."

Then she is falling, down and down through images and feelings that touch her and leave their scars on her. Sara's stomach flips over, her feet are hollow, and the nightmares flicker on and off in her blood and bones. Every sick image or idea she has ever repressed glimmers around her, through her. She is drowning in a sea of bad dreams.

Then the random images withdraw and she stands in the emergency room where she had her hands treated. In the dream, it is not daylight. It is night-time, and the rooms are empty: unattended, free of furniture. Just the sound of a heartrate monitor somewhere in the distance. Sara opens doors, looks in room after room. All empty.

Then a little groan. Her body prickles with fear. The squeak of a wheelchair. She turns, dread under her skin. In the wheelchair is Bonnie, the queen bee she beat to a pulp at sixteen. Her eyes are swollen, her nose bloody, her body hunched over on itself. The guilt winds her.

"I'm sorry, Bonnie," she says, but her words won't emerge from her throat, and Bonnie wheels her chair away down the corridor as though she hasn't even seen Sara.

Sara follows her, then sees a shadow move in the glass transom of another door. She opens it, and sitting on the floor is Dillon. His hair is lank and his eyes are shadowed: he looks as though he has lost every last shred of joy.

"I'm sorry, Dillon," she says. Again, he doesn't hear her. Room after room, and in each one she finds the people she hurt—emotionally and physically—her mother, her grandmother, the puppy whose leg she accidentally broke at age five, an entire room full of baby chickens that she had mishandled throughout kindergarten and at petting zoos. She understood now. She had always been a monster.

"Wake up!" she tells herself.

"Sara?" This is Ben's voice, from behind another door. She runs towards it and opens it. He stands in the dim room, cold moonlight splashed on the grimy tiled floor.

"Ben?" she asks. "Are you dreaming this too?"

"I can't wake up," he says. "I can't wake up and I have this feeling . . . Something bad is going to happen."

"Don't be scared," she says. "Whatever comes, I can kill it. I haven't failed yet."

"How can you kill it in your dreams?"

The scene dissolves and she is falling through the sea of dreams again. Time passes, slipping through her fingertips. When the images coalesce again, she finds herself hovering in the dark corner of a room. The walls are crude wood. There is a smell of woodsmoke and fish. She tries to move but cannot. Ben is nowhere to be seen, but in the room, beside a rudimentary firepit on the floor, are a fair-haired woman and a little boy of about eight.

134

They are talking in a strange language, and Sara watches. Long minutes stretch out and nothing happens. They talk, they eat, they get ready for bed. Sara doesn't mind: it's better than the dreams about dead chickens.

But then the door slams inwards, letting in a blast of snow. The woman stands to close it, but a moment later, Odin is there.

"Odin!" Sara calls. "Father!"

Odin doesn't hear her, and she is aware that she is watching a scene that unfolded a thousand years ago, because now the woman is standing Sara can see she is pregnant, and Odin advances on her with his hands around the curve of her belly. The woman shakes her head and cries and shouts, but Odin's words are clear enough to decipher. "Minn dottir. Minn dottir."

My daughter.

This is the night of Sara's birth.

The woman is forced onto the floor by Odin's powerful body. The young boy screams in fear and distress, pulling at Odin's clothes and futilely punching his meaty arms. Odin brushes him off as he might brush off a fly, and the boy lands on his backside next to the fire. Sara cannot see what is happening beyond Odin's hulking shoulders, but there is a spreading pool of blood, and white light brighter than lightning, and the awful howls of the woman.

Then she is suddenly silent. Odin stands and shifts a blanket over her body. The boy falls to the ground next to his dead mother and sobs.

"Oh, god, wake me up. Please. Wake me up," Sara says inside her head.

A voice rattles into her brain. Sara thinks it might be the voice of the old woman in her dream. "Look," it says. "Look at the boy."

But Sara doesn't want to look at the boy, whose face is smeared in his mother's blood. She struggles against sleep, but it is like pulling herself out of cement. The room dissolves and she is back with the old woman again.

"Am I entertaining you?" she says to Sara.

"Wake up!" she screams inside her head.

Ben is calling from far away. "Help me, Sara. Help me."

"The boy in your dream had terrible nightmares after your mother's death," the old woman says. "He visited me often. Often enough that we became friends. I'm a powerful magician, girl."

Sara doesn't know what all this means, but she knows that somewhere Ben is in trouble and she needs to wake up. Her dream self leaps on Mara, but the woman fades and disappears. The scene dissolves and Sara stands outside on a rocky plain, an icy wind flowing around her. She can hear the sea in the distance; a cold, grey sound. The air is foggy and sodden. She recognises it instantly as Asgard, another shard of its rough splendour, but this time it isn't a vision on the defeat of her opponent, she is here in a dream over which she has no control.

"Come back and fight me!" she calls.

Something huge and jagged thuds into her back. Sara falls to one knee and looks around. A rock lies on the ground next to her. Another hurtles towards her, striking her forehead and making her see stars.

She climbs to her feet unsteadily. "Come out where I can see you." Blood trickles over her eyebrow.

Thud. Another rock, this time in her shoulder. Mara's voice on the wind: "I'm over here with Ben."

Sara searches around with her eyes, sees and ducks another rock that speeds out of the mist with thundering power. Is she to stand here and be pelted to death? She can't fight what she cannot see.

The next rock that flies into her chest is four hand spans across. It knocks her over on her back and pins her down. Her breath leaves her. She gasps for air.

I must wake up. She'll kill me in my dream.

Sara tries to ignore the pain in her chest, the compression in her lungs. She reaches her mind out for the hotel room, the brown blankets, the dark furniture, the faraway sirens. Struggling against her eyelids, trying to move her hands.

Hauling herself up through the heavy, grey fog.

A gasp. Her gasp. The pain in her chest excruciating. Opening her eyes. Dark room . . . .

A hag sat on top of her, long white hair tickling Sara's face. One of the hag's knees was on her sternum, the other on the inside of her elbow. And her lips were very close to Sara's lips, sucking the air as it escaped from her mouth. Her wizened lips puckered hideously.

Sara brought up her free arm and punched the hag hard in the side of her head. The hag dropped off her to the floor, began to scurry, hunched over, towards the window.

Sara leapt up off the bed and seized her by the knees, bringing her down to the floor. Mara was just an old woman, didn't have any fight in her. Sara pinned her to the ground, their positions now reversed. She closed her hands around the hag's scrawny neck and Mara began to cough. Sara pressed harder. The hag opened her mouth, and out popped a glowing white bubble, that floated up towards the ceiling.

Then the hag disappeared.

Sara stood, turned towards Ben, who was lying motionless on the bed, his brown hair in strange tangled skeins.

"Oh, no. Oh, no, no," Sara said, switching on the lamp. He was pale but his skin was still warm. She slapped him gently. "Wake up, Ben. Wake up," she said, shaking him.

The white bubble floated down towards her, stopped and hovered in front of her eyes. Without thinking, she grabbed it and forced it into Ben's mouth.

He made a gurgling noise, then his lungs drew down and air rushed into his nose and mouth. A few seconds later, he started to cough, sat up and opened his eyes.

"What happened?" he said.

"I got her."

Sara and Ben both craved bright light and noise, so they pulled on their coats and walked two blocks to the all-night pizza café on Earl Street. The restaurant was inside an old, deconsecrated church, with polished cement floors and dark wooden furniture. It was a favourite haunt for drunken nightclubbers, whose harsh laughter echoed around the vaulted ceilings. Sara and Ben found a booth in the back corner and picked half-heartedly at a triple pepperoni special. Ben was pale, his face seemed sunken somehow, but she didn't know if it was an after-effect of Mara sucking out his soul, or simple fear. His fingers kept going back to his hair, unwinding the knots that Mara had twisted in it.

"So we need to talk about what just happened," Sara said at length, after the silence had stretched out a long time.

"We do?"

"You look . . . haunted."

Ben opened his mouth as if to say something, then snapped it shut again. His jaw was held tight, evidence that he was holding back some greater, unsayable feeling. He reached for his satchel and tipped up its contents on the table. "All this shit," he said. "Trying to find ghosts and monsters. Getting myself excited about the smallest piece of evidence. I feel like an idiot."

"But at least you've confirmed that there *are* supernatural things in the world. That feels good, doesn't it?"

"Yes, but they aren't able to be explored or contained. I'm so weak. I'm so . . . " He held out his skinny arms for a moment. "Mortal."

Sara didn't know what to say so she said nothing. Because it was true. He was so mortal. She could feel his difference from her acutely. He was a butterfly, his wings would shred on a cruel wind. The thought made her shudder.

He didn't see it. "I suppose I should thank you for saving my life," he said.

"I'm dangerous to you," she said.

"I'm not afraid."

"Perhaps you should be." She thought about Odin in her vision, the ruthless single-mindedness with which he had killed the Viking woman while the little boy sobbed next to her. This was her blood. This was what she moved towards.

"I need to tell you what I saw," she said.

"Go on."

Sara told him about the dreams she'd had while under Mara's influence, particularly the dream of her own birth. "I think the Viking is that little boy," she finished, and saying the words "little boy" out loud made her frightened of herself, frightened of what she might be capable of once she had stepped into Asgard.

"Obviously. And Mara has transported him through time to take up his blood feud."

"So why hasn't he tried to kill me already?"

"He's afraid of you." Ben shrugged. "Who wouldn't be?"

Sara considered him, eyebrows drawn. "Are you?"

"I'd be afraid to try to kill you."

"He has to try it sooner or later. He had a chance, when I was at the bus stop with my eyes closed. He could have slipped out a knife and—"

Ben bolted upright. "Oh. No."

"What?"

"He's too afraid to take you on. Of course. Even with your eyes closed, he'd be afraid you'd open them and see him and rip his head off. Sara, he's not going to try to kill you."

"What's he here for, then?"

"He thinks you killed his mother."

"Yeah, so . . . "

"Blood feud. He's going to pay you back."

Realisation was on her in a hot flash. "Mother," she gasped.

The mobile reception in the old church was terrible, so they went outside onto the dark street. Sara forgot that it was three a.m. The phone was ringing at the other end before anything as inconsequential as waking somebody up had occurred to her. But she didn't wake Mother up; because of course Mother wasn't home. As Pete told her helpfully on the answering machine their holiday ended in five days.

Sara slid her phone back in her pocket with a curse. "Not there," she said.

"Do you want to go over there?"

"They're overseas. Back Monday." She sat down heavily on the long aluminium bench of a bus shelter.

"She's safe for now then," Ben said. "What do you want to do?"

"I want to find the Viking," she said. "I want to find him and I want to stop him hurting my mother."

"How can I help?" Ben asked.

She considered him standing there in front of her. A streetlight reflected in the lenses of his glasses. "You've done enough. I've already put you in danger twice—"

"I put *myself* in danger at least once," he interrupted.

She continued as though she hadn't heard him. "I don't want to put you in danger again. I've got the Viking to contend with, and two more of Odin's monsters. You should just stay away from me."

"What if I don't want to stay away from you?"

"Look, I don't know what you think this relationship is . . . "

"This relationship isn't anything," he said. "I just want a taste of that world you belong to. I just want my life to be something . . . more. Please, let it be something more, even if it's only for a little while."

Sara folded forward, hands on knees. This wasn't how it was supposed to be. The day she'd run from her wedding was meant to be her last day here in Midgard, her last day worrying about others and what they thought and felt, her last day with ties to anyone. How had she become so knotted up again?

"Sara?"

"I don't know how to find him."

"I have eyes all over the city."

"Then yes," she said, exhaling, "you can help. But you have to do what I say, and if I say stand down, you must stand down."

141

"I can do that."

Where was she to find the Viking? Every time she'd seen him he'd been in a different place; he'd found her. She spent the day dazed and tired, wandering around the streets near her hotel, her gaze catching on every man with blond hair who moved past her. She ached with the city's vastness, its indistinct edges, its swarming multitudes. Street after street, alley after alley, in and out of shops, bars, cafés, cinemas, train stations, hotel foyers, and all the vast public spaces with their undifferentiated crowds of faces. No Viking. Not anywhere.

Sara found herself outside Cyrena's building, exhausted and gritty, at three in the afternoon. She knew she should be sleeping but it seemed far more important that she find the Viking, and Cyrena had helped once before. She buzzed and Cyrena's voice came over the intercom.

"Yes?"

"It's Sara. Ben's friend."

The lock clicked and the door swung in.

Cyrena was waiting for her with the door to her apartment open. "Welcome back."

"Thanks for seeing me."

Cyrena stood aside and let her in. "Any friend of Ben's is a friend of mine. Especially one as special as you." Her warm eyes crinkled at the corners.

"It's not a social visit," Sara said. "Sorry. I'm here because I want something."

"And I want to give it to you. But do let me make you tea."

"Do you have coffee?"

"Is instant all right?"

Sara nearly told her she'd eat it with a spoon out of the jar, she was so tired. "Of course it's all right. Thanks so much."

She waited in the lounge room but didn't sit down in case she accidentally fell asleep. Instead, she paced the perimeter of the room, stopping to look at the postcards. It seemed Cyrena had been to every spiritual sacred site in the world.

"You've travelled a lot," she called out.

"I have. I wanted to see it all." She emerged from the kitchen with two mugs. "I don't know if Ben told you but I have a tumour sitting on my brain."

Sara turned, took the mug gratefully. "Yeah, he did mention it."

"For whatever reason, it's taking a long time to kill me. I'm fitting in everything I can. Shall we sit down?"

Sara sat on the couch, Cyrena next to her.

"Ben's very fond of you," Cyrena said.

"Did he tell you that or did you figure it out psychically?"

"Neither. I see how he looks at you."

"He's a good person. But I'm not around here for long."

"He's always been special. He used to come home from school with me because I lived next door. I'd make him afternoon tea and help him with his homework, and he was always such a calm little thing, with his skinny hands and curls." She smiled. "He has a special heart."

"Don't worry, I'm not going to break it. He knows we're just friends." She sipped the coffee gratefully. "He said you weren't always a psychic."

"It's technically not true," she admitted. "I'd always had strange feelings about things, and sometimes dreams that turned out to be prophetic. But I kept it locked up inside. My mother would have been ashamed of me."

Sara sniffed a bitter laugh. "I hear you."

"Once the tumour developed, it all became supercharged. The world became brighter, sharper. I could see the tissue connecting us all. I could close my eyes and feel its contours." She closed her eyes a moment as though she were demonstrating, then opened them again. "It'll kill me though. I'm not delusional. I won't escape death."

"Nobody does," Sara said, shrugging.

"You might."

"Last time we spoke, you told me about my brother."

"I remember."

"I need to find him."

Cyrena put her mug down on the cluttered coffee table. "Come on, then. Give me your hands."

Sara chugged down half of her coffee then put her mug aside and laid her hands on Cyrena's. Cyrena's eyes closed and a silent stillness descended on them. Sara breathed slowly.

"He isn't in this world." Then Cyrena frowned. "Except when he is."

That made no sense, but Sara was too polite to point it out.

"In and out he goes. Through a door. A door he had to make himself with . . . nightmares."

Sara's senses prickled. She remembered what Mara had said, that the Viking had allied with her after his mother's death.

"There is so much malice in his heart," Cyrena continued. "He is sick with it. He has found a place here in Midgard . . . I can't see it,

144

because he is in it but he is deep within it. Hidden inside the way dark thoughts hide in the mind. But he has come here through nightmares, ridden them as a ship rides ocean currents. Childish nightmares, the worst kind."

"I'm so sorry, Cyrena, but I don't follow."

She cracked one eye open. "Nor do I, dear. It's a jumble. Give me a few more moments."

Sara waited.

Cyrena sighed and withdrew her hands, opening her eyes and reaching for the coffee mug. "Sorry. He's slipped beyond my sight."

"So do you have any idea where I should start looking for him?"

"None at all. When he's in his hole, I can't see him."

"Could he be travelling between now and his own time?"

"Indeed, yes. But he needs a place to arrive. There is a place here in this world, but I couldn't get a fix on it. I kept seeing flashes of children having bad dreams . . . I'm sorry, it's not much to go on. Perhaps you could think about where children have bad dreams?"

"But that's anywhere," Sara said. "He could be anywhere."

Ben showed up at work that night and slipped her a slender book. "I haven't heard anything from my sources yet," he shouted over the loud music, "but I thought this book might help."

She turned it over. *Mythology of the Vikings*. "Thanks, Ben," she said close to his ear.

"I haven't given up. I won't give up."

"I know you won't."

Back in her bed at the Inchcolm Hotel, Sara flipped through the book. She found Mara and read about her: a demon who stole the souls of the living while they slept, often taking the form of an old yet freakishly strong hag.

Not that strong.

Sara let the book fall on the covers beside her. Closed her eyes for just a moment, and fell asleep with the lamp on, the weariness of her day claiming her. Dreamless for hours. But it was still dark outside when she woke to a light thud just outside her door. She clung to sleep, sliding back under long enough to see and feel fiery runes that spelled out DRAUGR, leaving a stinging pain in their wake.

Sara sat up. Her heart was hot. Number six was here.

She flung back the covers. Her discarded clothes nearly tripped her on her way across the floor. She jerked the door open. Nothing. She looked down one side of the hallway and then the other. Brown carpet and flickering fluorescent lights.

But then she looked down. A damp pool on the carpet and a stick of some kind. She bent to pick it up and realised as soon as her hand closed over it that it was Heithr's staff, the one she had thrown into the river. Something had retrieved it.

Sara took it into her room and closed the door. She considered the staff carefully, shuddering lightly as she recognised the familiar pattern of human skin. There were no messages or clues on the staff; it looked exactly as it had the day she had thrown it away. She propped it up against her dresser and turned to the book Ben had given her.

Draugr. A revenant spirit, usually of a drowned man, who seeks to take the living into his watery grave with him.

She skimmed through the entry, her eye catching on the last line. *Lore holds that a draugr may be destroyed with fire.*

A slither and a thump in the hallway. The sound of a door further up opening and closing with a soft snick.

Sara pulled on her dressing gown and emerged from her room, checked the hallway was clear and headed for the stairs. The hotel was silent except for her hurried footsteps. She arrived on the lower floor and lifted the heavy gate that separated the reception counter from the foyer. Behind here, she knew she'd find the kitchen. One door, marked PRIVATE, clearly led to Neville's flat. She tried the other door and found it locked. Quietly, she focussed her strength and popped the door handle out of its lodging. The door swung in.

The kitchen was in darkness. She felt about for a light switch and the room was momentarily flooded with light, then browned out, then light again. A yeasty smell, the rattle of an old fridge. She crouched down and opened cupboards one by one. Old rusty tins of cooking oil, bags of spices and sugar. She pushed them all aside, couldn't find what she was looking for. Sara stood up and reached for a high cupboard over the fridge, pulled down a wire tray. As she did so, a white first aid tin dropped on her head then clattered to the floor. Bandages and headache tablets spilled everywhere. But in the wire tray she found a can of fly spray. Tucking the fly spray into the front pocket of her robe, she switched everything off and closed the door behind her and left the mess behind. Perhaps she would explain to Neville tomorrow: no hotelier wanted a draugr hanging around in his rooms.

Underneath the reception counter she found Neville's cigarette lighter. Armed now, she climbed back up to the fourth floor and began to creep along the corridor, listening at each door. At the third door along, under a dead fluorescent bulb, she paused. A ragged breathing noise on the other side. Her hand went slowly, silently to the door handle. It would be locked. She'd have to smash it and push the door in with one movement to catch the draugr unawares.

With sudden force, she squeezed the handle, feeling it disintegrate in her fingers, and kicked the door in.

The lamp was on. She could see straight away there was no draugr here. Instead, in the bed was a middle-aged man pleasuring himself.

"What the fuck!" he shouted.

"Sorry!" she said, making a show of averting her eyes as she backed out. "Sorry, sorry!"

Then she closed the door behind her and hurried up the hall. Stop, listen. Nothing. Stop, listen. Nothing. And then . . . water. Running, overflowing, splashing.

"Hey. Hey you." It was the man from the other room, dressed now and ploughing down the hall, fists clenched.

"Sh!" she motioned to him.

"No, I won't be quiet. Who do you think . . . ?"

She leapt towards him, wrenching his arm behind his back and clamping her hand over his mouth. He folded in pain and she released her grip a little, reminding herself he was mortal and too easily hurt. She pressed her mouth up to his ear. "Shut up, okay? Go back to your room. Don't look. You're safer that way."

He struggled once more but she tightened her grip. He slumped his shoulders in surrender, nodded, and she released him roughly. He spat, glared at her. She shooed him away and she recognised the effort it took him not to shout at her, not to puff out his chest and dominate the space with his hard, hairy male body, but instead to silently slink off to his room.

Sara returned to the sound of running water. She tried the handle.

Unlocked. Gently, she pushed the door open. It swung inwards, a band of grimy light falling on the carpet. The room was identical to hers, except reversed: bed against the left wall, dresser against the right. The same framed picture—an abstract nude lying in a field of poppies and daisies—hung over the dresser, but was askew. Sara reached out and straightened it. A digital clock on the bedside table flashed the figures 12:00 over and over. The light was on in the bathroom, the door pulled to. A puddle of water emerged from under it. Sara tiptoed across the carpet, stopped just outside the bathroom, put an eye up to the crack and peered in.

Only a strip of the scene was visible to her. Under bright bathroom light, a thing was flopping around on the floor. It was pale grey, human shaped, but tangled in fine weed and mottled with algae. A horror to behold, but she had lost the ability to be horrified. With her own deadly arms, what was the difference between her and them? She had been created out of blood and terror; that she knew now as a fact. She was not so very different from this monster in front of her.

The bath was filled and overflowing, and the draugr appeared to be rolling for pleasure in the water across the tiles. Sara almost felt sorry for it. Almost.

Sara took the fly spray in one hand and the lighter in the other and kicked the door open.

The draugr looked up with milky, horrible eyes. Snarled. Climbed half to its flipper-feet.

Sara pressed the button, lit up the fly spray like a blow torch, and turned its full fiery force on the draugr. An oily, burning stink filled the room. The creature screamed and threw itself into the bath, displacing a huge wave of water and extinguishing its burning skin. Sara cast the fly spray aside and lunged forward, grabbing the draugr around its neck and hauling it above the water to punch its face. Her right foot skidded on the wet floor and she wobbled forward. The draugr's hand was around her wrist in a second, tight seaweedy ropes shooting from its fingers and tangling her limbs. It pulled her into the water and she went in head first, banging her shoulder on the side of the bath. The thing wriggled out from under her, slippery as an eel, and she felt more ropes of seaweed encircling her. She struggled against them, felt some snap as others entangled her. Her lungs were bursting. She kicked against the back of the bath with her legs and managed to get her nose and mouth out of the water, though now her arms were behind her, her skin burning against her bonds. The draugr leaned over her and licked the side of her face.

Sara flung her head back with force, heard the crunching bone of the creature's nose. It recoiled just enough for her to free her arms. She grasped the edge of the bath, hauled herself out while the draugr tried to tangle her legs and trip her. She kicked its seaweed ropes off, stumbling and grabbing at the side of the toilet to keep herself upright. Then turned and slammed both arms into the draugr, taking it down to the wet floor.

"She went in here."

"What's going on?"

Voices in the hotel room. Her masturbating friend had gone for help. She couldn't think about that right now. The thing kept shooting seaweed ropes around her arms and wrists and neck, and she had to keep snapping them off.

"Fuck off, Spiderman," she grunted as she slammed its head into the tiles, again and again and again.

"Oh my God!"

"What is that?"

She had an audience. Sara grabbed the draugr's ears and smashed its head as hard as she could on the watery floor.

This time it was the sea. Beneath her feet, round stones and long ribbons of crinkled seaweed. Above her, a cloudless vaulted sky of pale blue. The pounding grey ocean beat its ancient ponderous rhythm, as though it was saying, "Mm, hush," over and over; a parent's words to a child who had grown upset over some tiny thing. She felt her smallness, her own inconsequential anxieties, dissolve and wash away in the thunderous sound of this grey ocean.

"I am weary," she said. "I am so weary." And she wanted to stay, here at this exquisite, rough edge of the world, where she could see and hear and taste the sea and the sky blurring into each other at some distant, unreachable horizon.

Sara almost forgot herself back in the hotel room, the draugr's head being beat over and over against the tiles. But then she saw her own bloody hands and she was back just as the creature blinked out of existence.

She slumped over, panting and coughing, pulling off seaweed. Its smell reminded her of her vision, and she had to haul herself into low-ceilinged Midgard reality, compress her spirit back inside her mortal-for-now body.

"What the hell was that?" This was Neville's voice, panic making it shrieky.

She turned her sodden head towards him. "A monster. I killed it for you."

Neville's eyes rolled back in his head, and he began to fall, his hand clutching at his heart. The masturbating man caught him.

Time to call an ambulance.

CHAPTER THREE

TIME ENOUGH
FOR EVERYTHING

SARA NOW HAD A PROBLEM SHE HADN'T
anticipated before. She sat in the back of the
ambulance, Neville's fingers clutching her hand
in a death grasp, and turned it over in her mind. She had defeated
six of Odin's seven challenges; one to go. If it came today, or any
time in the days before her mother got home, it would be too soon.
She didn't know what would happen when she defeated the final
monster. Would she magically transcend Midgard with no way of getting back to save her mother? Odin had said time passed differently
in Asgard. A moment there, while she sought permission to return,
might mean a year had passed here; her mother might already be cold
in her grave.

It became impossible the longer she pondered it: she needed to be out in the world in order to find the Viking; but being out in the world increased her chance of finding the last challenge.

The young paramedic who was treating Neville as they bumped over city streets took off his stethoscope and turned to her with a smile. "The good news is it wasn't a heart attack," he said.

"No?"

The paramedic patted Neville's shoulder. "Just a panic attack. Can happen to the best of us. We'll still take you to the hospital, get it all checked out."

Behind his oxygen mask, Neville looked relieved. He nodded once at the paramedic, then turned his eyes to Sara. His lips formed the words, "what was . . . ?"

Sara leaned close, spoke directly into his ear. She could smell his soap, his oily hair. "It doesn't matter," she said. "Whatever comes, I can kill it. You're safe."

His eyes fluttered closed. She suspected her words weren't much comfort.

Sara sat by the window of her hotel room, watching the alley below. Hoping he would come again, so she could catch him, crush him, keep him away from her mother. But the Viking didn't come, as she knew he wouldn't. Last time she'd seen him, she had led him to Mother's house. That was all he needed. Wherever he was now—in the city or in the sky—he knew better than to get too close to Sara.

Day and night had ceased to exist for Sara. The clock on her phone told her it was two in the afternoon, but there was so little light in the alleyway and her sleep had been so disjointed that it may as well have been two in the morning.

A light knock at the door sent a spike of adrenalin to her heart. She opened it warily.

"Ben."

"You look relieved," he said, closing the door behind him.

"I defeated another monster. Last night. This morning. One left."

"That's great."

"No it's not. I have to stay here and protect my mother. Here in Midgard I mean. Not here in this hotel. I'm pretty sure I'm going to get kicked out soon."

"Why?"

"I trashed a bathroom killing a draugr."

Ben barely blinked. "I've got a few leads on your Viking, but I don't know how helpful they'll be."

Sara sat heavily on the bed. "Go on then."

"Blond guy in Viking clothes spotted riding the B-line train, and again by another of my contacts who was standing on a platform out past Zone 3."

"The B-line doesn't go to Zone 3."

"That's right. Maybe he's just travelling around, keeping moving. Or maybe he was going somewhere. Or lost."

"Viking on a train." She smiled grudgingly. "Sounds like the name of a crappy movie."

Ben laughed. "Action flick or romance?"

"Comedy," she said. "I've had enough of the others."

"Anyway," he said, "I've got all my spies looking."

"How many spies do you have?"

"Not that many. But my spies have spies, if you know what I mean. The word is out there."

"I don't have long. Days."

He perched on the edge of the dresser. "Sara, there's one place you'll definitely find him."

"What do you mean?"

"He has to go to your mother's house. Eventually."

She turned this thought over. "But I won't be there to protect her."

"There's a way you can be."

She met his gaze. "Okay, then. Show me."

He stood, reached for her hand. "Come on."

They climbed into a cab outside the hotel, and Ben directed the driver to Mother's street in Harmony Square.

"How do you know her address?" Sara asked.

"I did some database searches on you," he admitted sheepishly. "Before I knew you better. You've got to understand, I'm a researcher by vocation. I hope you don't mind."

"I have bigger things than my privacy to worry about," she said, shrugging.

"I found your wedding notice. It listed her address. I've already been out there once. That's how I know."

"Know what?"

"Just let me show you."

The cab rattled over the bridge and back towards the Square. The road ran alongside the forest and she watched it blur past, light-shade-light. Above the grey-green treetops, the sky seemed too blue. Her heart ached unexpectedly for the ordinary earthly beauty she would leave behind.

She turned her head and glanced across at Ben. He was looking at her with unabashed admiration. She had to smile. He checked himself and turned his attention to his satchel, making himself busy with his mobile phone.

The cab dropped them off outside Mother's house. Sara stood on the grassy verge and waited while Ben paid the driver, wondering why he had brought her here. Her pulse thudded in her throat. A chorus of rosellas clattered in the trees. In the City, birds never sang. Everything about Harmony Square was so familiar, so soft and pretty. She had thought this life was behind her, and she had burned her last bridge on the way out of it.

"This way," Ben said, gently grasping her upper arm and turning her away from Mother's house. The cab rattled off with a belch of acrid blue smoke, as Ben led her to a house diagonally opposite Mother's. The grass in the front garden was long and weeds ran rampant in the flower beds. Amidst it sat a FOR SALE sign, with a faded sticker peeling off it. Sara smoothed out the sticker and read it. UNDER CONTRACT.

"Whose house is this?" she asked.

"Nobody's by the look of it," he said, going up to the front window and peering in. "Look. Completely empty."

Sara joined him, put her face up to the window. Inside were bare, beige carpets.

"The view from these windows," he said.

"Straight across to Mother's house."

"When she comes back, we can watch over her. When the Viking comes . . ."

157

"What makes you think he's going to use the front door?"

"He might. But if he doesn't . . . well, we are going to warn her, aren't we?"

Sara's mind reeled. See Mother again? Talk to her? "It won't come to that," she said firmly. "I'll find him before he finds her." She strode to the front door and took the handle in her hand, but Ben stopped her.

"Back door," he said. As he did so, she became aware of the occasional passing luxury car. "Not out in the open."

She followed him around the side gate and to the back door. A clothes line sagged violently to the right, faded pegs still clipped to the nylon. At the back door, a broken bucket waited, filling with rain and leaves.

"I'm amazed somebody hasn't complained about how this place looks," Sara said, cracking the lock with a quick swipe of her knuckles. She pushed the door in. The house smelled of trapped air and, faintly, lavender. They moved through the silent kitchen into a large living room. The beige carpet was clean, but faded in shapes around invisible furniture. She tried the lightswitch and nothing happened. She was about to curse when a dozen expensive downlights flared into life. "Electricity is still on."

"Perfect for squatters," Ben said. He moved to the front windows and pulled the curtains on both, leaving the one nearest the door apart about an inch. "Look, it's an uninterrupted view."

She joined him at the window, leaning her head against his long enough to see Mother's house in the slice of view the curtains let in. A moment later, in a blur, his lips were on hers. She stood back. "Hey! No!"

"I'm sorry," he said, flushing beet red.

"You just like me because I'm a freak," she said dimissively, breaking eye contact, moving to the other window.

"That's not true."

She let the conversation slide. She had bigger things to worry about.

Neville sprang up from behind the counter as she entered the hotel.

"You're back!" she said. "Are you okay?"

"Fine. They had me on a heart monitor overnight but decided it was just . . . shock."

"I'm really sorry."

"You have to go."

She sighed. She could have guessed this was coming. "I won't be here much longer, I promise. I—"

"You have to go," he said more forcefully. "I've seen some shit in my time, but never . . . " He shook his head and his mouth worked in a way that suggested he was trying not to cry.

She pointedly looked away. "It's all right. I understand."

"You're paid up until the end of the week. I'll refund you."

"Keep the money. I don't need money where I'm going." She headed to the stairs and up the dark stairwell. Passed a maintenance man fixing the lock on one of the doors she'd broken down. Sara packed her last few possessions in a bag. She thought about phoning Ally, telling her she wasn't ever coming back to work. But then surmised that Ally would figure that out when she didn't show up for another night.

"Do you have somewhere to go?" Neville said to her as she crossed the foyer.

"Yeah. Kind of." She opened the door, stepped out into the spring sunshine, then let it close behind her.

Ben was at the empty house, unrolling power cords and plugging in lamps and a kettle. He'd shopped too: instant noodles and packet soup.

"Not my first stake-out," he explained. "There's sleeping bags upstairs in one of the bedrooms. I don't know how long we'll be here. Until we're kicked out, I expect."

"Or until the Viking comes," Sara said.

"Do you know what time your mother's flight gets in on Monday?"

"No. What day is it?"

"Friday."

Her heartbeat hitched. "Seriously?" Perhaps she wouldn't find the Viking first, perhaps the showdown was going to take place in her mother's house. "Maybe he'll come tonight. Maybe he comes every few days to check, and we'll see him and . . . that will be that."

He stopped in his unfurling of extension leads and studied her a moment. "What does that feel like?" he asked.

"What?"

"To know you can just . . . you know. Defeat anything."

"I don't know that."

"Six supernatural creatures, sent from Asgard. Every one of them."

"There's always the seventh," she joked grimly.

"Go on. Tell me."

She took a deep breath. She wasn't good at capturing feelings in words, let alone talking about them. "I've always felt the strength in me, as if it's buried in secret places between my bones and blood. Just

160

a little coaxing and it squeezes out into my limbs and it feels . . . wonderful to let it free. Imagine if you had to curl up tight in a ball for hours and then you could simply stand up."

"Yeah, I can imagine that."

"But the more I do it, the further I get on this path to Asgard, the more I can feel that I'm becoming something else."

"Becoming what?"

"One of them. One of the things I'm fighting. A monster."

"You're not a monster."

"I'm not a human anymore. Not fully. My Asgard blood is cold and a little cruel. I know now that it's always been in me and I've done things . . . " She trailed off. "I can feel that side of me intensifying, swamping me. I don't know what I'll be once I get there, once I've been there a long time. Maybe I'll be like my father." She thought about the Viking as a little boy, seeing his mother ripped apart. "I don't know that I want to be that . . . deadly. That ruthless."

"You'll be who you are," Ben said. "You're half-human. You just have to hang on to that aspect of yourself."

Something about his hopeful voice, his turn to bright platitudes, made her feel even more monstrous. She wanted to tell him that it was such a mortal thing to say, but she didn't. "Maybe you're right," she said instead.

That night, she took the first watch while Ben slept upstairs. Sitting by the window, one elbow leaning on the sill, chin cupped in her hand. She watched her mother's house and her mind wandered, back to her childhood, back to her adolescence. All those years she hadn't known about her true provenance, about what was coming. Had she been better off then? The quiet beyond the window was soothing after weeks in the city. The night was velvet, soft and dark. She was conscious of feeling a sense of peace, despite everything that weighed upon her, and she wondered if it was simply being close to her mother's house that gave her that feeling.

Dawn came to Mother's street and as it did, a familiar car pulled into sight. Sara sat up, heart fluttering. It was Pete's car. They were back early.

"Ben!" she called. "Ben, come quickly."

Ben stumbled down the stairs a few moments later, looking bleary. "What? What is it?"

She watched the garage door open, swallow the car, and close again. "They're back."

There was no point in resisting. She had to go and speak to her mother, and she couldn't delay a second. Perhaps the Viking had been watching too, from somewhere Sara couldn't see.

"Will you come in with me?" she asked Ben.

"If you want . . . do you think I'll be welcome?"

"I don't even know if *I'll* be welcome." How on earth was she to return? Especially now she was so close to escaping for good: only one of Odin's challenges to go.

"Welcome or not," Ben said, "you have to warn her."

She grasped his hand and squeezed it tight. "Come on," she said.

They crossed the road. Sara stood at the front door a few moments catching her breath, then raised her hand and pressed the doorbell.

She could hear it deep inside the house, could imagine the warm scent of the rooms, the soft light in the lounge room. Time passed. Then the door opened. It was Sara's stepfather, Pete, in a rumpled tracksuit and with his silver hair unkempt.

"Sara?"

"I need to see my mother."

"What? We've just endured a seventeen hour flight. You can't just—"

"Please. I know you're angry, but I need to see her. It's an emergency."

Pete glanced at Ben, then back to Sara. "Wait here," he said, and closed the door.

Sara turned to Ben. "What will I do if she won't see me?"

"Phone her? Write her a note? Don't worry, she'll see you."

She glanced around her, at the freshly stained decking and the tidy vines of Chinese jasmine climbing the trellis and the terra cotta bird bath. A bird twittered in the trees. All so familiar and so ordinary. After the unfamiliar and extraordinary things she had seen and done since leaving Harmony Square, the moment seemed surreal.

The door opened again. Mother stood there, her hair neatly plaited and her travelling clothes miraculously crisp. Her mouth was pressed in a line, working against some unreadable emotion. Pete stood behind her, hand protectively on her shoulder.

"Mother," Sara said, "you're in danger."

"What?"

"I need to come in and talk to you."

"Who's he?"

Sara glanced at Ben and back to Mother. "This is my friend Ben."

"Is that why you left Dillon? For this . . . pipsqueak?"

"Um . . . maybe I should go," said Ben.

"Please, Mother. Let us in. I have . . . so many things to explain to you."

Pete squeezed Mother's shoulder. "Maybe you should listen to her."

Mother glanced up at Pete. She looked momentarily like a little girl, uncertain and looking for reassurance.

"I'm so sorry about what's happened," Sara said, "and I will try to explain everything if you just let me in."

"All right," Mother said grudgingly.

Sara followed her mother inside, Ben trailing uncomfortably behind her. In the lounge room, Pete drew the heavy brocaded curtains, admitting golden morning light. The setting was achingly familiar: the tick of the carriage clock on the mantelpiece, the smell of fabric softener in the throw over the sofa. *Home, I am home.*

"I'll make coffee," Pete said, excusing himself.

Sara sat on the floral lazy-boy, Ben perched on the arm. Mother settled herself on the couch, self-consciously touching her hair. She didn't like to be seen without make-up.

"I wouldn't have come back if it wasn't important," Sara said.

"Do you have any idea how worried I've been?" Mother said.

Sara spoke over the top of her. "You're in terrible danger."

"What nonsense." But it sounded brittle, afraid, and Sara understood: years of self-delusion, years of glossing over her strange daughter's provenance and abilities, were about to be swept away. Mother was holding as tightly as she could to her denial, but it was crumbling through her fingers. She would go down fighting; Sara knew that.

"I know you don't want to hear all this, but you must listen. I've seen things . . . " Sara trailed off, not sure how to frame her warning to get under her mother's defences.

164

"You've seen things?" Mother gave Ben an imperious once-over. "Is that right?"

Sara ignored her. "There's a man who's been following me. He knows where you live and I think he wants to kill you."

"Are you involved with drugs?"

"No."

"Then why would . . . ?" Mother put her face in her hands a few moments, breathing deeply. From the kitchen came the sound of Pete frothing milk on the cappuccino machine.

"You have to get out of here," Sara said. "If I can find him, I can stop him before he gets to you, but—"

Mother's head snapped up. "Will you listen to yourself? A few months ago I would never have heard such rubbish from you. Are you deluded?" A sharp intake of breath; her voice became soft. "Are you mentally ill?" Her voice grew surer, happier, as she imagined herself back on stable ground. "That's it, isn't it? You need help? I'll pay for a specialist."

"I'm not crazy. I'm . . . Mother, I found my father."

"You don't have—"

"Everybody has a father except Jesus, and I'm far from Jesus," Sara shouted. "Stop saying I don't. I've met him. It's Odin, the Viking god."

An expression of frigid horror crossed her face, and Sara wondered if Mother was remembering something, some terrifying truth that she had buried long ago.

"Mother? Are you all right."

"Get out," she said through bloodless lips.

"Please, please. You and Pete have been away a few weeks, go for a few more. Just until I sort this out."

Mother began to sob and shout. "Go. Leave me. I don't want you in my life. I don't want this in my life. Go. GO!"

"But Mother, I—"

Ben grabbed Sara's arm. "Come on, Sara."

Sara flicked him off and he staggered back and fell into the sideboard with a great clatter and crash of plates falling over.

"I can't leave. She'll die!" Sara shouted.

Ben righted himself, dropped his voice low. "This isn't helping. She won't listen. We'll find another way."

Sara's face worked against sobs. "I don't want her to die."

Ben pulled her gently towards the door. Mother slammed it behind them.

Halfway across the road, Pete called out to her.

"Sara! Sara, wait!"

She stopped in the middle of the road, and he caught up to her.

"I heard only some of that," he said.

"I don't need you to berate me," she said.

"I'm not, I'm . . . I'm not an idiot, Sara. As much as your mother has tried to hide things from me, I'm aware that you're . . . as you are. But it caused her such anxiety. She's been better without you here. I know you don't want to hear that."

"I care only for her safety."

"She's in danger?"

Sara nodded, and Pete's brow creased. "I lose nothing from believing you."

A Volkswagen backed out of the next-door driveway, nearly

reversing into them. Sara took a few steps towards the gutter and Pete joined her.

"I'll call a security company," he said. "The moment businesses open. I'll have them out here as soon as they can get here. Tomorrow. Today if possible."

Sara's stomach unclenched. "You will?"

"Absolutely."

"I'm watching too," she said, indicating the house across the road.

He nodded. "Between us, we can keep her safe." He lowered his voice. "She has nightmares, Sara. She never remembers them but I hear her shouting and crying, saying, 'there's so much blood,' over and over. Something dark happened to her that she's forgotten or tried to forget. I often wondered if she was raped, if that's how you were conceived."

Sara's eyes went back to the house, as the circumstances of her conception and birth flashed across her mind. She was born of a bloody blackness; how did she expect to be anything else than the thing she was. "Look after her, Pete. I loved her so much. She was everything to me."

"You were everything to her," he said.

"But times change," Sara replied.

"Yes, they do," he said. "Don't worry. I'll take care."

Sara had never felt more acutely her outsideness, her radical difference from Harmony Square and all that lived there. Sitting by the window in the still, silent, empty house, watching through a gap between curtains. The sun moved west and shot a yellow-gold beam sidelong past her eyes, a beam that illuminated drifting dust motes behind her. Ben worked on his laptop for part of the day, occasionally saying, "hmmm", occasionally bringing her black coffee, then finally going up to bed just on dusk to sleep for a while before his watch.

His watch. She wouldn't let him watch. Only she could watch. She trusted no other eyes but hers.

But as the night wore on, as the lights went out in her mother's house across the street, her eyelids grew leaden. She closed them for a moment, imagining Mother getting ready for bed, plaiting her hair, cleaning her teeth. Would she think over their exchange from this morning and say to herself, *perhaps I will be careful, just in case?* Double check the doors were locked; keep her phone close to the bed; lie in the dark a while listening for strange noises? Sara opened her eyes and fixed them on the house across the street again. She hoped so. She hoped it so hard her ribs ached.

Around three in the morning, Ben came down. "Go get some sleep," he said.

"I won't sleep. I'll worry."

"If I see anything, anything at all, I'll scream so loud it will wake you."

"Anything, okay? If a twig so much as quivers . . . "

"I'll wake you. I know how much this means to you."

Sara glanced back out the window.

"Is there something else?" Ben said.

"I'm afraid of sleeping. Not just because I'm afraid of taking my eyes off her house. I'm afraid of dreaming the final runes, of the final challenge coming before I save her."

He nodded, his glasses glinting with reflected streetlight. "Maybe, if it comes, you can just run away from it for a while."

"I guess so." She thought about the challenges so far, about the possibility of other people getting hurt.

He touched her shoulder gently. "Maybe it won't happen. But if you don't sleep, you'll be tired and weak."

She smiled grimly. "I'm never weak."

Sara climbed the stairs and wriggled into one of the sleeping bags. She lay there a while, her body tensed. This was madness. She wouldn't be able to sleep. She should move the sleeping bag downstairs, sleep in the corner of the lounge room with Ben. That way if anything happened, she'd be close by.

But the heavy tiredness in her limbs and mind conspired against her, and she plummeted into sleep.

A long darkness ensued, then began to shred apart and lift away. Behind it, a fiery light. The runes. She struggled to wake herself up before she saw them, but there was only one. Not a name, just a letter. Perhaps not even a letter: a burning arrow, pointing directly upwards, its point seeming to burrow into the soft tissue of her brain and lodge itself there, throbbing painfully. Somewhere, from the conscious part of her mind, she interpreted it as the rune equivalent to the letter T. T what?

Sleep wrapped around her again, taking her down dark corridors. She was looking for her father. If she found him, she could ask him what to do. Behind shadows she searched for him, then standing in dark spaces that doubled back on themselves into malleable infinity, shouting his name over and over. "Odin! Odin!"

Breath in her head. A face swam across it. The blond man, his mouth grim. The Viking.

"Where is your mother?" he asked.

Then she shocked awake, white-hot adrenalin sharp in her heart. She scrambled up, feet tangling around the sleeping bag, then thundered down the stairs.

"Ben?" Surely it was just a dream. He would be there, smiling at her bemusedly.

But he wasn't there, nor was he in the kitchen, nor any other room. She flung the curtain aside, accidentally pulling the curtain rod and fixtures out of the wall. Plaster rained down on her. Lights were on at Mother's house. What had happened?

She ran to the front door and wrenched it open, nearly tripped over Ben who was lying in a bloody heap on the front step.

"Ben!" she cried, skidding to her knees and turning him over.

"I'm sorry, Sara," he managed, through bleeding lips. His glasses were broken, one eye already swelling up blackly. "I'm so sorry."

IV UNCLE T

"Cattle die, kinsmen die,

the self must also die;

but glory never dies . . . "

—*Havamál*

CHAPTER ONE

MOTHER

WHEN THE BLACKEST MOMENTS unfold, there is a little pause in the progression of things: a held breath, an arrested beat of the heart, a gap in reality—a pin's width across—where nothing makes sense and so nothing matters. Sara held as tight as she could to that pause, but even with her godlike grip it slipped away, and noise and pain rushed into the vacuum. She helped Ben to sit up but it was clear he was terribly injured, his shirt soaked with blood.

"Can you breathe okay?" she asked him.

"I need an ambulance."

She handed him her mobile phone. "I'll be right back." Then she was sprinting across the road. Her mother's front door was open, the lights all blazing. Somewhere within, a man was sobbing. She raced up the stairs to find Pete sitting on the bed, in his striped pyjamas, his grey hair in disarray and his gnarled hands over his face. She had never seen him look so old.

"Pete?" she asked, alarm making her voice shrill. "Where's Mother?"

"He took her," he said into his hands. "I couldn't save her. He hit me over the head . . . I think I blacked out for a while. But I saw him . . . he held a knife to her throat, he dragged her away." He descended again into sobs, all the more awful because they were the evidence of a man in his sixties, one of the calmest men she knew, completely losing his composure.

"Oh, Christ," Sara muttered, frozen with helplessness and indecision, her skin hot and clammy.

"I called the police," he said. "They should be on their way."

"The police can't help," she retorted. "Do you not understand? This man is not from our time. He could have taken her anywhere." Sara told herself to think straight; at least Mother was alive. If he'd intended to make good on his blood feud, he might have killed her right away. For some reason he hadn't, and that meant hope still existed.

Pete leapt to his feet, handed Sara his car keys. "You can save her, can't you?"

Sara set her mouth. "Yeah. Yeah, I can. And I will. Just watch me."

Sara left her mother's house, and sat on the dewy grass with Ben. The sound of distant sirens reminded her of the City and its grim unpredictability. Harmony Square wasn't meant to be like this.

"Are you going to die?" she asked him plainly. She needed to prepare herself.

"Nah," he said. "I'm a wuss. I ran before he could work me over more seriously. Sorry."

"What happened?"

"I saw him, bold as brass, walking up to your mother's house."

"If it had been me on watch . . ."

"Maybe you would have fallen asleep on the job and neither of us would have seen anything."

She shrugged, didn't want to say anything further in case Ben took offence.

"I ran out and tried to take him down, but he took me down in a second. I called, but you mustn't have heard. When he came back with your mother, he kicked me a few times. I played dead."

"Was Mother . . . did she say anything?"

"She was crying but it was soft. He had her under his arm. I think he had a knife."

Sara's eyes fluttered close, an unbearable echo of her mother's vulnerability sliding across her skin.

She opened them to a sea of flashing lights: the police and ambulance arriving at the same time. "What do I do, Ben? Where do I look for her?"

"It's one in the morning. The guy's a Viking. He can't drive a car, he can't hail a cab, and the buses are stopped for the night. He has to take her to his hiding hole, and he's been seen around trains."

Sara climbed to her feet, galvanised. "Okay. I'm taking Pete's car to the train station." She turned back to him. "When you get patched up, call me."

"You'll need this," he said, handing her mobile phone back. "Mine's inside on the charger."

175

"Call me," she said again.

"I will."

She pulled up Pete's Mercedes at the nearest train station, locked it, and pocketed the keys. The platform was empty, dark except for a single light over the name of the station. As she approached, even that snuffed out. She waited for the next train, her panic itching in her legs, fighting the notion that this course of action was futile.

Minutes passed. The light above her flared into life again, and she regarded it for a moment, until it burned a yellow bar on her field of vision and she had to look away and blink.

Electricity. When Odin came, it went out. Four frost giants had also plunged her into darkness. Not the troll nor the draugr, but she'd fought Modgudr and Mara in the dark. The strength, the intensity of their supernatural force, seemed to predict whether or not the mundane systems of Midgard were disrupted. And now, increasingly it was she who was disrupting them. She was becoming more of that other place than her own world. The thought terrified her and thrilled her.

In the distance, the howl of an approaching train. The blast of cold air ahead of it had her stepping backwards on the platform. She stepped into a brightly lit but completely empty carriage, and the doors slid shut behind her.

As the train sped ahead, she walked through the carriage and pushed the button for the door to the next one. She was briefly in the loud, dark connecting carriage, then back in the bright passenger area. Another empty carriage. She continued down through the train. A young couple, kissing violently. An Asian woman in a dark uniform, on the way home from a night shift. A sleeping drunkard. No Mother. No Viking. She came to the last carriage and sat down heavily. If she rode all the way to the interchange, she could get on another train, do another walk-through. Maybe she could ask people if they'd seen them: a fierce-looking blond man and a pretty middle-aged woman who might be frightened, who might be struggling to stay calm. Who might be crying, as Ben said, softly.

The train stopped at a station. New passengers. She rose half-out of her seat, ready to walk through again. But then the train went dead. All lights blinked out. The doors, in emergency mode, slid open and stayed open, allowing a cool breeze to lick over the tops of the seats and lift her hair. A strange silence pressed on her hearing, as though all noise were muffled by some invisible pillow of air around her ears. She became aware that her heart was thudding, alert to something primal that her brain had not yet caught up to.

Sara caught her breath and waited. Dark. Still. Perhaps in other carriages people were muttering to each other in disquietude, a driver was calling an emergency number for advice, the drunkard was rousing from the sudden withdrawal of noise. Moments passed, a minute, two . . .

Then light and movement. The sound of the airconditioning exhaling. The doors slid shut and the train started again.

It was on board. Whatever thing it was that her father had sent, the unnamed thing starting with T; it was on board and it was coming for her.

Her muscles filled with liquid fire: her body preparing for a battle that she had consciously decided not to fight. She had to get off the train before it came. If she defeated it, she might not get a chance to save Mother.

The train hummed into a tunnel. She could see her own frightened face reflected in the window. She rose and stood near the door, willing the station to come soon. The door between carriages opened. She turned.

A man walked in. She knew straightaway he was her next challenge, and she was confused. He didn't look as formidable an opponent as she'd been expecting. Just an ordinary man in his fifties, with a neat beard, and dressed in leather and fur. A little soft around the middle. He only had one arm. An empty sleeve was pinned across his chest.

He would be too easy to defeat. She had to get off.

He approached her with a grim smile. "Sara?"

"No," she said. "You have the wrong person."

He laughed and said something in a language she didn't understand. She shrugged theatrically. "I don't understand, sorry."

"Of course you understand. You're one of us." And somehow, the words reached her ears and made sense. She could hear that he was still speaking the strange language but now she understood it perfectly. "I said you smell like your father." He gave a little half-bow. "I'm Odin's cousin. Your uncle, in a way."

The train was pulling in to the station. She began to frantically hit the button to open the doors. "Stay away from me. I don't know who you are."

He spread his remaining hand to his side, palm out. "I'm your last challenge."

The door opened. She made to leap out, but he caught her by the arm and yanked her back. All her breath left her body. His arm was an iron bar. He held her up with one hand, and smashed her into the wall of the carriage. Her brain rattled in her head.

"Don't try to run away," he sneered, pulling her close to his face.

The pain in her arm almost turned her inside out. As though he was liquefying both muscle and bone. He held her balanced by it, her feet inches above the floor, without any effort at all. The soft alarm that let her know the doors were about to close sounded. She brought her free arm up and ploughed the heel of her palm into his face. It was enough to throw off his balance and he dropped her, falling against her. She scrambled from under him and out onto the platform. The door hissed shut behind her.

He punched through the window, but it was too late: the train was moving off and she was dashing across the platform for the train on the other side, leaping in and landing with a slide just as the doors closed and the train began to move. Across the platform she could see him, grim and staring back at her, until the trains moved apart and he was lost from sight.

Sara tried every train line that was running, walking up and down carriages asking if anyone had seen them. Nobody had. She called Ben just before two, as she arrived at the Interchange, certain that the Viking had gone to ground by now.

"Any luck?" he asked.

"Nothing," she said. "How are you?"

"I'm okay. I'm at Cyrena's now. All patched up and on some pretty strong painkllers. I think I've got something on your Viking."

"What? Where is he?"

"I don't know, but I have a clue."

Sirens in the distance, drawing closer.

"Okay, I'm coming. In the meantime, look something up for me. My last challenge found me. A cousin of Odin; name starts with T. I didn't dream the whole name . . . just a T." Two police cars and two ambulances screamed past, echoing in her phone harshly against her ear.

"Got it. I'll see what I can dig up," he said. "What's happening there?"

"I don't know . . ." Had somebody found a body? Was it Mother? The sirens had stopped near the Inchcolm. "I'm just going to go check it out, then I'll be with you. Hold tight."

"Be careful." Then he laughed at himself. "Not that anything can kill you."

She didn't tell him she'd found somebody who might. She pocketed her phone and headed towards the ambulances. Two young women were walking towards her. One was sobbing while the other one tried to comfort her.

"What is it?" Sara asked. "What's happening down there?

The non-sobbing girl looked up. "Some old guy's gone nuts at a bar near the interchange. Must be on ice or something. He's taken down a half-dozen people and locked himself in with the woman who runs the place."

"My boyfriend," the other girl sobbed. "He's all messed up. They wouldn't let me in the ambulance."

"It's okay," the friend said. "The train's just here. We'll be there in no time."

"Which bar?" Sara said, but she knew. She knew.

180

"*Ally's Alley,*" the girl said.

Sara started to run, three blocks in zero seconds.

Red and blue lights flashed grimly in the dark. Police were already moving roadblocks into place. Bloody and battered people on stretchers.

"Get out of the way!" a paramedic yelled at her as she pushed through.

A police officer with a short-back-and-sides haircut stopped her. "Whoa, whoa, love. You can't go in there."

"Is it a man with one arm?"

His expression twitched. "I'm not at liberty to—"

"Is it a man with one arm? Wearing leather and fur? Yes or no?"

"You don't demand answers from me, miss."

Sara tried to use words and ideas that he'd understand. "Look, the man in there is my uncle," she said. "And the woman he's holding hostage is my boss. You can't send me away. I can fix this."

"Your uncle?" His eyes went over her head, to where an unmarked car stood. A woman in a dark coat was climbing out. Sara presumed she was some kind of hostage negotiator or detective.

"Yes," she said.

"Wait here. I'm going to find you somebody to talk to." He beckoned to another police officer. "Don't let her over the cordon."

Sara watched him go, eyed the other police officer. They weren't going to let her in. They were going to ask her pointless questions, probably back at a police station miles from here.

She ran.

"Hey!" the police officer shouted.

But she darted down an alley. She knew the back way, where the

181

delivery drivers came in, and she wasn't going to wait for any of these breath-and-dust mortals to let her do what she was meant to do.

Sara doubled back and found the laneway the delivery trucks took. She ran up the hill, then into the narrow drive where she had first met Ally. Empty kegs stood guard around the security door, reinforced and three inches thick. Sara cracked her elbow down on the handle and it popped off. She stood back and kicked at the door. It thundered in the quiet alley and she knew the police on the other side would hear it and figure out something was happening back here. She had to be quick.

She picked up an empty keg and tried using it as a battering ram, but it crushed like an empty softdrink can. So she used her shoulder, slamming it into the door, feeling the door's weight and its resistance, then the first faint yield. Once more, running up, slamming into it.

It buckled. She kicked the lock, felt it warp underneath the arch of her foot. A second later, the door was hanging bent on its hinges, wide open.

There was little point in trying to be quiet. She ran through the storeroom and into the main bar area, where Ally sat on the stage with her head between her fluorescent pink knees while Uncle T stood over the top of her, his left foot resting on her upper back. In the dim glow of the security lights over the bar, they were as still as statues.

Then Uncle T came alive and nodded at her. "You came. I thought you might."

"Let her go."

Her uncle stood back. Ally straightened, saw Sara and said, "Thank God."

"Go," Sara said to Ally. "The back door is open."

182

Ally didn't need to be told twice. She raced past, leaving Sara facing her uncle.

"I can't do this right now," she said to him.

"What do you mean?"

"I have to save my mother first. If I fight you now and I win, there might not be time to find her."

"If you fight me now and you die, then nobody will find her."

"Yeah. That's it." She allowed herself a little hope that he would understand, that the fact that they were kin—however remote—would mean something.

"But you'll be too dead to care."

"I want her to live for her sake. Not for mine."

"These Midgard attachments make you weak," Uncle T said. "To my advantage."

He began to walk towards her and her heart picked up its rhythm. "No," she said. "Please. Not now."

"We don't get to choose when we face our challenges," he said. "Life is rather messier than that. You are the strongest woman on earth. Fight me." His arm shot out—that iron limb that had held her in the train—and she ducked just in time so that the punch skimmed over the top of her skull instead of mashing her face. Even so, the blow made her cry out. She scrambled away on all fours, only to find herself being dragged back by her right ankle. Sara kicked out wildly, then wrenched herself over onto her back. He struggled to maintain his grip on her ankle, bent down to right himself, and she took the opportunity to kick him squarely in the face.

He stumbled back. She got to her feet and ran.

He was after her in a moment, of course. A monster made of heavy iron, thudding on the pavement as she ran. But she knew the City in a way he didn't, she knew the labrynthine alleys and drives around Ally's bar, and she put on a burst of speed and ducked between them, down them, over a fence and up a fire escape, smashing her way into the back door of an old hotel. The security alarm blared into life, but she had lost him. She caught her breath, then leisurely made her way down with the guests fleeing their rooms in alarm to assemble in their pyjamas just outside the foyer. She slipped off down Baron Street, and caught a train to Cyrena's.

CHAPTER TWO
DAUGHTER

"I HOPED I MIGHT SEE YOU AGAIN," Cyrena said to Sara. "Come in. Sit down."

Ben was half-lying on the red couch, so she sat next to him.

"Hi," he said weakly. Without his glasses on, he looked as vulnerable as a turtle without its shell. In a different life, they might have been good for each other. Two gentle souls who didn't quite fit anywhere.

"You okay?"

"Painkillers are wearing off. But I'm okay. I found out about your uncle."

Cyrena hovered. "Should I make tea?"

"I don't think we have time for tea," Ben said.

"Ah. Well." She sat down next to Sara, fixing her in her gaze. Her pupils shrank dramatically and suddenly. "You're on your way out of this world," she said.

"Yes, I don't think there's long."

"I won't see you again with these eyes," Cyrena said.

Weary sadness washed over Sara, but she told herself not to feel it. "My uncle," she said to Ben. "We just did some family bonding. Tell me about him."

"Tyr," Ben said. "He has his own rune. War god."

A war god. For the first time, it occurred to Sara that she might not defeat this one, that she might actually die. *On your way out of this world.* She had spent so long being invincible, she didn't know how to feel. The fear of her mother's death was still stronger than fear of her own.

"You said you had a clue about the Viking's whereabouts?" Sara asked.

"The paramedic that treated me knew me from hanging around the emergency clinic. He told me that yesterday morning, around this time, he'd stitched up a man who said he'd been thrashed by a blond man in weird clothes and a plaited beard, had his wallet stolen. Our Viking."

Sara's body went on alert. "Where did this happen?"

"Out near the rail terminus. Zone 3, Sara. That's two people have seen him around there. It's a big area, but it narrows our search."

Sara pushed a finger gently into Ben's shoulder. "You're not searching. You're not coming."

"You can't leave me out of it now. I didn't even need stitches. I'll be perfectly fine."

Sara turned to Cyrena. "Is he lying?"

"Ben's not given to lying," she said with a warm smile.

"Cyrena, can you try again?" Ben asked. "Any clue at all about Sara's Viking friend?"

"He's not my friend," Sara muttered.

"He's good at hiding himself," Cyrena said.

"But this time you're not looking for him alone. You're looking for Sara's mother."

"I can try," Cyrena said.

A hot star of panic touched Sara's heart. What if Cyrena could see her mother was dead? What if it was too late?

But Cyrena had her hands out, palms up again. "Come on, Sara," she said.

Sara laid down her hands.

Cyrena closed her eyes, and Sara watched as her face twitched with concentration. "Think about your mother, Sara. The stronger I feel her, the easier it will be to find her."

So Sara did what she had been avoiding for ages. She closed her eyes and she remembered the love between her and her mother. Early morning cuddles and help with maths homework and singing in the kitchen and the two of them for dinner, the two of them against the world for such a long time. She had been a cuckoo in her mother's nest, but Mother had loved her just the same.

"She's alive," Cyrena gasped.

Sara dropped her head. *Thank God.*

"She's alive because he wants her alive," Cyrena said. "I'm getting a clear fix on him now. He wants to hurt her and frighten her before he kills her. Once he has settled the blood feud, he will flicker out into nothing. He knows this. He will put off the death for a long time."

"I have to find him," Sara said. "Before he hurts her."

"He has already hurt her," Cyrena said, opening her eyes. "He will want you to know that she suffered. You must be quick."

"Where are they?" Sara demanded. "Can you see them?"

Cyrena lowered her eyelids again, dropped her head, breathed deeply. The room was silent. Ben sat motionless, a held breath nearby. "I see a long stone building," Cyrena said. "Dilapidated. Abandoned."

"Where is it? Can you give me a street name? A landmark?"

"I can hear trains," she said. "I'm sorry, I'm trying as hard as I can."

Sara forced her pulse to slow down. She would find him and she would kill him and her mother's suffering would be over. Horrible images flitted around the edges of her mind, but she wouldn't let them in. Whatever her mother was experiencing, it would end soon. She would make sure of it.

"The house is old," Cyrena said at last. "Red brick. Two storeys high. I can see it from outside now. Dirt where there should be grass. Weeds in all the flower beds. The constant sound of trains." She opened her eyes again, and shook her head. "That's all I can say. I can see it clearly in my mind's eye, but I can't give you an address."

"We'll find it," Ben said. "Come on."

Sara stood, but Cyrena tugged her hand to hold her still a moment. "A shadow follows you. Stone and steel."

"I know." Sara stopped herself from asking if he was going to kill her. "It's my uncle. Apparently."

"Keep moving. Make it hard for him to get a fix on you."

"Okay." She nodded. "Thanks. Take care."

"Goodbye," Cyrena said. "I was honoured to meet you."

They caught the train. It slid through tunnels and under bridges and out of the City, into cold breaking daylight and behind the houses of people who had long since grown used to sleeping through train noise. A long freight train blurred past them, its howling and rattling muffled by the double-glazed windows in their carriage. Sara rested her head on Ben's shoulder and he stroked her hair.

"We should be out to Zone 3 in twenty minutes," he said. "Why don't you close your eyes and rest?"

"Twenty minutes isn't worth it," she said. "I don't want to miss anything." Her eyes went to the window. Backs of dilapidated shops, tight alleyways, factories, high-density government housing, empty platforms so thick with graffitti that she couldn't name the stations. The train rocked along, and the motion was soothing.

"Listen, Sara," Ben said, all in a rush. "You'll be gone soon and I have to say something."

She straightened and turned her face to him. The bruises on his face were starting to bloom purple and yellow around his eye and cheek. "What is it?"

"I love you." He met her eyes briefly, then his gaze darted away. His face reddened.

"Ben, I'm so sorry."

"Kind of *not* the answer I wanted to hear."

189

"I'm sure you don't really love me. You don't even know me—"

"Don't tell me about my own heart," he said tersely.

"Sorry," she said again, returning her gaze to the window. A few minutes passed, and guilt and sadness burned in the space between them. "Ben," she said, face still turned away from him.

"Yes?"

"We would have been good together. If I'd stayed."

He didn't say anything, but she knew that he was smiling.

They hit Zone 3. The buildings had thinned and suburbs sped past, trees and parks and fences, all softened by early morning light. Perhaps these were the things she'd miss, eventually. The familiar would be beyond her reach. The thought gave her a hollow feeling in the arches of her feet.

Ben moved to the seat opposite and kept his eyes glued to the view. They were both looking for the same thing: an abandoned building on a dirt lot, red brick.

Occasionally, a building would flash past that fit some of the description, and she'd panic, worried Cyrena had got the detail wrong. She could see from the corner of her eye that Ben's body tensed from time to time too, and imagined he must feel the same way.

"Just make a note of the nearest station," she said. "We can always come back."

Zone 3 sprawled on. The train stopped at every station, but their carriage remained early morning empty. They were approaching the terminus now, and Sara's heart was falling and falling.

Until she saw it.

Behind the terminus buildings, on a hill that looked down onto the tangle of cables and the crisscross of train tracks, stood a red brick building with boarded-over windows.

"Ben!" she cried, and was waiting at the door before the train had stopped at the platform.

Sara pushed herself up the hill hard and fast, Ben trailing behind her. She had forgotten his wound from earlier. She was fixed only on one thing: rescuing her mother.

"Sara, wait!" Ben called.

"I can't wait," she said over her shoulder. "It's probably best if you don't come anyway."

"You can't just go barging in."

"Why not?" Barge in, find the Viking, crush him to dust. A simple plan.

Ben put on a burst of speed and caught her. "Because the moment he knows you're there he'll kill your mother."

Sara paused, turned to Ben in the soft blue morning light. He looked pale, apart from the contusions around his head, and he was doubled over slightly. "Pain killers wearing off?" she asked.

"Worn off," he said.

"I'm sorry." She glanced back at the building. "It's not safe for you, Ben."

"I want to help."

"You can't. You know you can't."

"Go in quietly," he said. "See him before he sees you."

She nodded. "Wait here. I'll come back for you."

191

"Good luck."

Sara nodded grimly, then headed back up the hill. The front fence of the building came into view. On the bricks, white letters that had been bolted there long ago. Some had fallen off.

ST MAR ARET'S ORP AN G.

St Margaret's orphanage. She remembered the news stories from twelve years ago, when she was still in high school. A scandal had erupted about crooked staff taking government money and letting the children starve and live in filth. The establishment had been closed down, but the building was surely full of children's nightmares.

Ben's advice was good. *See him before he sees you.* As she drew closer, she clung to the shadow of the neighbouring church, stopped between trees to peer out. Just because the windows were boarded over didn't mean he couldn't see her. He could be watching the front gate through a crack in the boards.

She decided to circle around, come up the back way.

Sara climbed over a chainlink fence, three doors down from the abandoned orphanage, and found herself in an empty lot. A faded sign said *Used Cars*, but the only evidence that cars had ever been here was the occasional oil stain on the gravel. She crunched across it as quietly as she could, found the back exit and emerged onto a new street. She counted back three houses, figured she now stood in front of the building that backed onto the house the Viking hid in. The building was an empty house, with all its windows broken. The cement slab it sat on was cracked with spiky yellow grass struggling through. She picked her way around the side until she came to the back fence.

She couldn't see over it, so she put her toe on the lowest crossbeam and carefully peered over. A huge, black tree with spiky green leaves dominated the back garden, and had stolen all the sun from the grass and the nutrients from the soil. The yard was dirt and rocks, an old incinerator, flower beds where weeds grew in profusion. She hoisted herself up, placed her feet on the upper crossbeam, and slid over the fence, lowering herself down behind the cover of the pine tree.

She waited here a moment, looking up at the building. A peeling green door hung ajar.

A rustle of wind howled through the branches of the pine and she took the opportunity to cross the dusty garden. Then stopped, back flattened against the bricks next to the green door. Waited. Her pulse thundering in her ears. She listened and heard nothing.

"I'm coming, Mother," she said under her breath, and pushed the door open.

Inside, it was dark and dusty. Her nose itched. Old carpet, threadbare and faded, under her feet. Peeling wallpaper. Mould blossomed on the ceiling. The door fell closed behind her, making her jump. She took a few steps in then stopped. To her right and left were rooms. One was obviously a kitchen, with mud in the sinks and rat nibbles out of the wooden benches. The other may have once been an office. Old folders lined sagging shelves. No Viking. No Mother.

Sara headed further into the building, checked in empty rooms, found nothing. A staircase ahead of her. She put one foot on the first stair and it creaked loudly. He would know she was here. She froze, heart thudding. Then leaned her weight on the banister and crept up the stairs as quietly as she could.

At the top of the stairs, she listened again. Nothing. She found herself at the head of a corridor. Wet stains had spread then dried on the wallpaper, which had faded from lavender to grey. No carpet up here, just bare wooden boards coated in dust. Two rows of doors, three on each side.

Behind one of them, he would be waiting. Did he already know she was here? Was he waiting for her to open the door so she could witness her mother's death, just as he had witnessed his own mother's?

The thought made her pulse with rage.

She whipped open the closest door. The room was empty. A single, thin beam of sunshine through a hole in the boards illuminated bent floorboards. She backed up. The next room. Again, empty. This time, it was clear she'd found a bathroom, with four shower cubicles lined up one next to the other, and rusting taps and fittings jutting from the walls as though frozen with rigor mortis.

Again and again she opened doors, until she came to the last one. She pressed her ear against it and heard nothing. The rage kindled. Now she could kill him. Now she could smash him into oblivion for hurting her mother.

She kicked open the door.

No Viking.

The room was long and thin, with five rusted beds on either side. Rats had eaten the mattresses and left piles of droppings everywhere. She walked between them. A board was missing, allowing in enough light through the grimy glass to illuminate the miserable remains of a dormitory where orphans had once slept. Once dreamed.

Where was he? Where was Mother?

Sara stood in the centre of the room and closed her eyes. A cold breeze ran across her skin and she breathed it gratefully, then her eyes flew open. There were no open windows, nowhere for a breeze to come from. Was there a hidden door? She felt along the walls, high and low, but found nothing.

She sat on the edge of one of the beds and thought about the children who had suffered here. Orphans, like the Viking. Young, defenceless, seeing things children should never see. Dreaming at night and waking up to a sustained nightmare in the morning.

The Viking had been only a child when a monster had walked in and killed his mother in a flurry of screams and dark blood. And that monster was her father.

The rage inside her dwindled, flickered like a candle at the end of its wick. So she was still human after all. She hung her head. "Mother, where are you?"

The breeze again. She lifted her head. There on the wall, right between the beds, was a door she hadn't seen before. A door that hadn't been *there* before. And it was open.

Sara stood and walked through it.

She found herself in a wooden hut, with a low ceiling and rough-hewn walls. A square fire pit sat in the middle of the room, with an empty pot hung over it. The fire was low. No chimney sucked out the smoke. Rather, it filled the room and escaped eventually from a small hole in the wooden roof. Pots and spoons and spatulas hung over the fire. Bunches of dried herbs hung from the roof beams. Benches were built into the walls at knee height, and one of them had a bundle of rough blankets on it. Another had a grinding stone, a sack of grain. Windows were shuttered with wood, and a door was an inch ajar. Through the gap, she could see a forest.

Sara glanced behind her, could still see the empty beds beyond the doorway she'd come through. She turned her attention back to the wooden hut and knew that she was in the Viking's world now, in his time, in his home. She knew she needed to go outside and find him, but was afraid to leave the doorway back to her own time.

But if she was afraid, then Mother would be infinitely more so. With a deep breath, she pushed the door open and strode out into the past.

Almost immediately she heard it: her mother crying for help. Hoarse and shrill. "Help me, help me!" she called. Sara entered the trees, following her voice.

It stopped but Sara tramped on through the forest all the same. A frigid wind whipped at her spring-time clothes, made her skin rise in goosebumps. The forest floor was damp and mossy, and she slipped and caught herself on a rock, cutting her palm open.

"Help me!" came the cry again.

Sara reoriented herself, picked her way between the tall spruce and birch. The breeze ran past again, rattling branches.

Then she could hear him, talking in a low voice to Mother. At first it was a jumble of sounds, but then, as it had with Tyr, the language broke on her ears and made sense. "You'll die no matter how much you shout," he said, and then she saw them.

Mother was tied to a tree, the Viking stood in front of her with a large knife. Blood smeared Mother's hands, her clothes were shredded and bloody. Neither of them had seen her yet. She ducked behind a bush, picked up a rock and threw it a hundred metres away.

She could see the Viking's head turn. "What's that?"

"Sara?" Mother called, and it hurt Sara's heart to think that Mother had hoped she'd come for her.

The Viking grunted then headed off in the direction of the noise. Sara dashed to the tree, signalling to Mother that she must be quiet.

"Get me out of here!" Mother shrieked. "I want to go home." Her voice sounded wild and desparate, harsh against Sara's ears. Sara was used to Mother making only soft, contained noises. Her reality warped.

"Sh," Sara said, snapping the bonds that held her mother to the tree, watching her hands as if they didn't belong to her.

"Don't tell me to shush!"

The commotion brought the Viking back. His footsteps came thundering through the forest. With an unholy howl, the Viking barrelled towards them, arm raised with a knife, and Sara knew that he would die trying to plunge that blade into her mother's heart.

He was mortal; he would die easily.

But that part of her that wanted to remain human didn't want to kill him. She stood between him and Mother and caught his arms the way another woman might catch the arms of a child. It would be so easy to crush his bones and sinews, but she forced all her might back inside.

"Stop," she said in his language. "I'm sorry. I'm so sorry for what my father did."

"Your father is scum. You are scum," he spat.

She could feel movement behind her, and realised her mother was pulling off her ropes. She willed her not to move, to stay behind Sara where she was safe.

"You don't have to do this," Sara said. "We are brother and sister."

"You are Odin's girl," he said. "You are the reason my mother died."

197

Mother slipped out from behind her and ran. She turned, distracted, and he wrenched himself out of her grasp, lifted the knife to throw it.

"Mother! No!"

She whipped around, knocked his hand so that the knife went wide of its target. Enraged, he went after Mother.

"Please," Sara said, but he wouldn't listen.

She turned her eyes heavenwards a second; something shifted inside of her. With a roar, she jumped on him, tackled him to the ground, buried her foot in his middle. He tried to push her off, but the molten rage had surged into her blood now and letting it flow made her feel like a god. She fell on top of him, pummelling his head with her fists, feeling his skull shatter and shard, pulping his face until long after he was dead, stopping only when she couldn't bear to look at it anymore. She remembered again the image of him as a child, and bile rose in her throat.

Sara sat back. She flipped him over, his blond hair bloody. She became aware of a shadow nearby. It was Mother, staring at her with cold dismay.

"I saved you," she said.

Mother closed her eyes.

The wind whipped up. Her skin turned to ice. "We have to get back," she said to Mother, climbing to her feet.

"Don't touch me!" Mother shouted, and Sara realised she was covered in the Viking's blood.

The ground began to shake.

"Mother, we have to go. I don't know how long that doorway will stand open."

Mother began to sob, her mouth gaping open in horror and pain.

Sara collected her in her arms and began to run. Through the trees, back the way she'd come, following the smell of smoke from the little hut. Mother pounded her fists on her, like a child having a tantrum. "What are you?" she said. "What is happening?"

"I'm your daughter and I'm getting you home," Sara said, running, thumping over rocks and roots, then bursting out into the open and across to the hut. It seemed to shudder in her vision, and she became afraid that it was going to disappear and leave her here in this ancient world where Mother would die from an infection in her injuries. She wrenched open the door. The ground juddered beneath her, began to peel away from her heels as though it was falling away. The door to the orphanage stood open, but it seemed further away the closer she moved towards it, receding into dim translucence.

"No!" she shouted, and put on a burst of speed. The floor fell away from her feet, she jumped.

Landed on the other side with Mother. When she turned around, the doorway was gone.

"Mother?" she said.

Mother was awake, but wouldn't answer.

The Viking had pulled out all Mother's toenails and fingernails, cut off the tips of both her ears, broken several of her ribs, and burned long blisters over her arms and back. Sara carried her down the steps and out the gate and down the hill to where Ben was waiting.

"She's going to need a hospital. I saw one back two stations."

"I want to go home," Mother cried, her first words since Sara brought her back to the here and now.

"Mum, you need medical attention."

"Let me go home to Harmony Square." Mother was wild-eyed, blood-smeared, her pulse thudding visibly in her throat. "I want to get away from here. I want Pete."

Sara turned to Ben. "Call a cab," she said. "We'll meet Pete at Harmony Private." She stroked Mother's hair. "You're going to be all right."

"What are you?" Mother asked again, her voice fearful and angry all at once.

"I'm Sara."

"You're a monster."

"I'm not a . . . " But Sara couldn't confidently finish the sentence.

The waiting area of the Harmony Private Hospital was thickly carpeted, with deep armchairs and a coffee machine, and a view out through floor-to-ceiling windows onto rolling grass and well-groomed trees. More like a country club than a hospital. Ben and Sara waited, as the sun came up bright and warm behind them, flooding the room with light.

Sara paced.

"She's safe now," Ben said, in a reassuring tone.

"I want to see her. Why won't Pete let me see her?"

"Be patient."

"I've been waiting an hour."

"Sara?"

Sara whirled around. Pete stood at the end of the corridor, beckoning her. When Ben stood, he pointed at him and said, "No, sit down. Just Sara."

"Of course," Ben muttered, chastened.

Sara followed Pete down the corridor, past rooms with lavender wallpaper that were filled with flowers. "What's taken so long? How is she?"

"She's scheduled for surgery this afternoon. One of her ribs is dangerously close to piercing a lung. She's full of painkillers at the moment but . . . she's asked not to see you."

Sara stopped in her tracks. "What? Then why . . . ?"

"I know she'll regret it. That's why I'm taking you in." He dropped his voice low. "The police have been. They've asked about you."

"I'm not afraid of the police, Pete."

"Just letting you know." He started walking again, then pushed in the door of the last room on the corridor. Shades were drawn over the sunny windows. Mother lay in a large bed with crisp white sheets, gazing at the ceiling.

"Mother?" Sara said.

She turned her head. Through the fog of painkillers, she scowled. "Not her," she said.

Sara advanced towards the bed, reached for her mother's hand.

Mother recoiled. "Don't you touch me."

"Please, dear," Pete said, sitting next to Mother and stroking her hand. "She's your daughter. You haven't seen her in months."

"She squashed his head," Mother slurred.

Pete's face showed his distaste.

"He was going to kill you," Sara protested.

"I told you to keep that thing inside of you," Mother said. "I told you nothing good would come of it."

Pete glanced up at Sara. "Perhaps this was a mistake. Perhaps you should come back later, after the surgery, when she's had time to get over the shock."

"Don't talk about me as if I'm not here," Mother said, though softly.

"There is no 'later,'" Sara said.

"Then don't come back."

Sara stood, uncertainly. Mother's eyes were closed now, as she drifted into a morphine-laced doze. Pete leaned over her, his love almost visible in the weak sunlight struggling through the blind. Sara longed to collapse and lie full-length next to Mother, to curl against her side, to take comfort from her touch as she had done so many times in her life. But Mother was all bones and spikes to her now.

She turned to the door. Nobody said goodbye.

Ben was nowhere in sight in the waiting room, but two police officers stood there waiting for her: a man and a woman.

"Sara Jones?" the woman asked.

"What is it?"

"We need to ask you some questions."

"Sure. Just a moment . . . nature calls."

"Wait . . . where are you . . . ?"

She kept walking, past them, into the ladies toilets. Pristine mirrors and bowls of pot pourri. She went to the last cubicle. The female police officer was behind her, but Sara locked the cubicle door, climbed up on the seat and pushed the aluminium window frame out of the wall. A second later she was running.

At the bottom of the path in front of the hospital she saw Ben, phone to his ear, pacing back and forth. When he saw her he beckoned urgently.

"What is it?" she asked.

"Cyrena called. She said somebody was trying to break in. The line went dead."

The heat in her blood again. "Let's go." She glanced back towards the hospital. "Fast."

Pete's car was still parked at the station, and Sara let Ben drive it to the City. They parked on the footpath outside Cyrena's building, half-blocking the bus lane. The City was coming alive. Coffee smells from cafés, traffic moving stop-start on intersections, cyclists whirring past on the way to pre-work showers.

Sara could see immediately that the security door on Cyrena's building had been wrenched off its hinges. Broken glass sprinkled the ground. They crunched over it and up the stairs. Ben pressed the lift button but Sara was too full of wild energy to wait for it. She began up the stairs, two at a time, heart pounding. At the thirteenth floor corridor, she could see already that Cyrena's door was open and light was spilling out.

She ran.

The scene inside Cyrena's tiny apartment was chaotic. The furniture up-ended, cushions and books scattered everywhere. She moved the objects, flinging them left and right. At the centre of the chaos, cold and still, was Cyrena.

Sara knelt, picked up Cyrena's limp arm to feel for a pulse. Tried again at her throat. Nothing. A bloody trickle from the corner of her mouth was the only outward sign that she had been hurt, but Sara suspected her uncle had splintered bones and crushed organs inside Cyrena's generous body.

Ben stumbled in behind her, saw Cyrena and called out, "No!"

"I'm so sorry, Ben," Sara said. "She's dead."

CHAPTER THREE
FATHER

K*EEP MOVING. MAKE IT HARD FOR him to get a fix on you.*

But she'd stayed too long at Cyrena's. Too long at the house near the train terminus. And far, far too long in the waiting room of Harmony Private.

Ben was bent over Cyrena's body, crying. She watched him at one remove, aware that her time in Midgard was streaking past her, remembering Tyr's warning that her attachments to people here were a weakness.

"Ben," she said gently, "I want you to take me back to the hospital, and then I want you to drive around and around and not stop anywhere until you're sure it's over."

He lifted his head, wiping his nose on his sleeve. "What? Why?"

"Because I don't want you to die. I don't want anyone I know and love to die. I need to go and face Tyr and have this over with."

"I want to be with you when you . . . finish."

She was already shaking her head. "No. No, you can't be. You're too mortal. You make me weak."

His face worked against his sadness and fear.

"I'm sorry, Ben, but you knew you would have to say goodbye soon."

He stood and moved towards her so fast she almost flinched. Then he pressed her against him and his lips were on hers and this time she didn't push him away, even gently. She let him bend her, as no man would ever bend her again.

When he stepped back he dropped his gaze. Sara pressed her fingers to her lips. They stood in that pose a few moments.

Finally, Sara said, "We should go."

Ben nodded. "I'll come back here later, let the police know."

"My fingerprints are all over everything here," she said with a shrug. "It's a good thing I won't be around much longer."

"I would have visited you in jail," Ben said with a weak smile.

"Like a few bars could keep me in," she replied. It was meant to be a joke, but it sounded very grim.

"Goodbye, Sara Jones," he said, holding out his hand for her to shake. "You were the most extraordinary woman I ever met."

"Goodbye, Ben Midnight," she replied. "You weren't so ordinary yourself."

If Tyr was tracing her footsteps, then he would have to go to the end of the train line and back before he came to the hospital. Even so, she approached the glass front doors warily. They slid open at her approach and she paused a moment, tensed. But it seemed everyone inside was alive, not cowering in fear behind reception desks and water coolers. She found a seat in the waiting room where she had spent an hour that morning and sat down.

The nurse behind the reception counter called out, "Visiting hours start at one."

Her mother was just a few hundred feet away. But Sara wouldn't be visiting her. "I'm just waiting for someone," she said.

The nurse looked at her warily, but didn't say anything else.

Oh, but she was weary. Weary and longing for it all to be over. She stared down at her sneakers, placed squarely on the pink carpet. A grey sadness entered her heart. For Mother, for Cyrena, for Ben. For Midgard.

Without realising, she nodded forward into a doze. Perhaps a few minutes long, perhaps a few seconds. Then started awake.

The light had changed. She looked up. The downlights above her were out. She leapt to her feet, turned her attention towards the glass front of the building. There he was, at the bottom of the path, making his way up, his face grey and forbidding. *Stone and steel.*

She ran towards the doors. The electric eye that opened them had blinked off with the electricity, so she wrenched them apart with her hands and barrelled towards him. If she didn't let him inside, he couldn't hurt anybody. The reception nurse. Pete. Mother.

Tyr had other ideas. As hard as she slammed into him, he slammed into her harder. She flew back, sailed through the glass with a deafening crash, then sat blinking among the gleaming debris.

The nurse screamed and ran. Sara put her hand up and grasped Tyr's ankle, tried to pull him down next to her. Instead, he kept walking, dragging her through broken glass that grated through her clothes and against her body. She climbed him, hand over hand, reaching around his throat with the crook of her elbow. With effort, he shrugged her off, turned and grasped her around the shoulders, slammed her once more to the ground.

A security guard emerged from one of the corridors, pointing a gun at them both.

"Get out!" Sara shouted. "You can't kill him, he's a god. Get out."

The security guard, a buff man in his thirties, ignored her. Pointed the gun at Tyr. When Tyr advanced on him, he pulled the trigger. The gunshot was deafening at close range and Sara cringed on the floor. She had no idea where the bullet went—maybe directly into Tyr's guts—but it made no difference. Her uncle advanced on the security guard, grabbed the barrel of his gun and squashed it in his big hand, then slammed him against the reception counter. The security guard slid to the ground like a rag doll.

Sara caught her breath, and the pain in her lungs alarmed her.

She scrambled to her feet, desperate to get away from the main thoroughfare. The gunshot was sure to have aroused attention. She didn't want anyone else to come and investigate and find themselves smashed to pieces by Tyr. She ran off down a linoleum corridor that led to a double-door marked *Medical Staff Only*, and pushed it open so hard it hung off its hinges. He was behind her, fast and heavy. On either side of her, there were operating theatres. The door to one stood open and she dashed inside, put herself behind one end of the operating table. The only light in the room came from the long corridor, where a window looked out over the gardens. Dark gathered in the corners.

He was there a second later, advancing on her. "Are you going to keep running away or are you going to fight me?" he asked, and he seemed genuinely puzzled.

"I'm going to fight you where nobody else will get hurt," she said.

"Why would you even care? These Midgard mortals live for an eye-blink then they're gone."

"I am from here," she said. "I'm one of them."

"No you aren't," he said. "You never were. You have Aesir blood. Nothing can kill you." He shrugged a little. "Except perhaps me."

With that he leapt over the table and ploughed into her, sending them both clattering into stainless steel tables and drawers assembled beneath blue sheets against the tiled walls. Sara landed a blow into his chest before he bore down on her, grabbed her head and began to slam it over and over into the tiles.

Her brain rattled. She pushed all her strength down into her hands and reached for the shoulder of his only arm, using it to pull him close enough to headbutt him, so hard that she saw stars.

He stumbled back far enough for her to get out from under him, skid to the other side of the room and grab a stainless steel chest of drawers. She picked it up and hurled it across the room at him. It caught him in the face and he went down to his knees. While he was down, she leapt towards him, holding his head for balance and kneeing him repeatedly in the chin.

Hot pain in her knee. He had sunk his teeth into her. She yelped; he grasped her around the hamstrings and flipped her over his back. She landed face down on the floor and then his foot was in the side of her head, kicking her until her ears rang and her skull swelled with heat. Every time she tried to get up he kicked her down again. She spat out a tooth. A long stream of blood and spit ran from her lip to the floor.

Everything grew blurry. The lights had come back on, sirens moaned distantly. Or maybe that was just the sound inside her skull. She was dying now. She knew it. The only thing that could kill her—one of her own kind—was killing her. She had failed Odin's challenges. Not only would she never see Asgard, she wouldn't even have the consolation of life in Midgard.

Sara closed her eyes.

Odin was there, in her mind's eye. She was momentarily relieved of pain, standing in velvety darkness with her father. Somewhere, a thousand miles away, the sun was about to rise. It robbed the stars of their gleam. A soft breeze ran down the hillside and across the long grass and she ached with it.

"Well?" he said.

"Am I here? Or is this an illusion like the other visions?"

"What do you think?"

"I think I'm dying," she replied.

"And will you die? For me? Will you give up your life to honour my name?"

Sara stared back at him. A sick thud sounded over and over in her head, and she knew it was Tyr's blows, back in the expensive private hospital in Harmony Square. "Is that what you want?" she asked Odin.

"That's what countless warriors have given me before you."

The rage that whirled up inside her was brighter and sharper than lightning. Was this Odin's real game? To tell her that Mother and Dillon didn't care about her strength and will, only to demand those very things from her for himself?

Sara was weary of being told what to do.

"No!" she shouted at him. "Fuck you! Fuck all of you! This is my life and I'll do as I fucking please, to honour my own name. For my own glory."

And she was back in the operating theatre having her head kicked in by Tyr.

She pushed back, got her hands underneath her. Shouldered off his next kick. Got to her knees, ignored the rolling table he smashed into her back. Stood up.

Roared.

He took a step back and she jumped on him, slammed him into the ground. Then rolled over and stumbled to the operating table, which was bolted to the ground on a thick metal pole. She snapped the pole, raised the table above her head and smacked it down onto him, leaping on top of it once, twice; hearing him groan and shout with pain under it. He pushed up, pushed the table and her off him. She stumbled back, lost her balance and fell on her backside. Scooted away as he came at her with his big iron hand.

She hit the wall, climbed to her feet and slid past him on his arm-less side. He turned and pursued her. A large round operating light on an extendable arm hung from the ceiling. She grabbed the arm and smashed the light into his face. Glass flew. He went down to his knees.

Ringing in her ears. Soft, musical ringing. In front of her, Tyr's bent back. She leaned forward to grab him, drag him to his feet, keep punching him. But her arms closed around nothing. He disappeared.

She stood. All around her broken and bent objects lay. Blood on the walls. She turned her hands over in front of her face. Raw and bloody. Breathed in. Pain. The lights flickered and went out again. From behind her, a male voice. "Well done."

Sara turned. Odin was there. She scowled. "I didn't think I'd see you again."

"Why would you think that?"

"Because I wasn't prepared to die for you."

He spread his hands. "I didn't ask you to. I was testing you, to see if you'd learned your lesson. And as you so beautifully pointed out, it is your life. At last."

Sara glared at him still, pain making her impatient. "A little encouragement might have helped."

"No. You feed off the anger. It was what you needed. You are at your strongest when you own your power."

She glanced around. "So is he dead?"

"Tyr? No. None of them are dead. Neither trolls nor giants nor draugrs nor nightmares. None of them. I have need of them all yet, but I watched all your battles and withdrew the enemy when the result was clear." He nodded at her with a warm smile. "I didn't think you'd defeat Tyr."

"Would you have let him kill me?"

"I couldn't have stopped him."

She nodded. "And will he be mad at me? When I get to Asgard?"

"Who knows? He's not a grudge holder and I think he'll understand. Why don't you ask him yourself? It's time for us to go."

A cold fear was spreading through Sara's stomach. "Already?"

"You aren't ready?"

"I'm . . . this is big. You know?"

"I know. I also know that the building is surrounded by police with guns, and I don't know if you could take a bullet quite as easily as Tyr. We should be going."

"My mother . . ."

"She'll never forget you."

"Will I be changed?" she asked desperately.

"You'll be more yourself than you ever have been."

"Will I remember my Midgard self?"

"Only if you want to." He closed his eye and lifted his face as though he were breathing in a breeze laced with the scent of summer flowers. "And you will see things. Deep fjords as dark as a raven's wing. Towering waterfalls of midnight blue. Skies woven of colours you haven't even imagined. And for the long nights, the warm hall. The music and the fire and the laughter of your companions." He opened his eye and fixed it on her. "You'll never feel longing again. I promise you." He extended his meaty hand. "Come, daughter."

She reached her bloody hand for his. "I'm so scared."

Her flesh met his. Light blurred all around her. "It only means you're alive," he said.

Crushing pressure swelled into her skull, then her body ran with heat, turned to sand. She surrendered, and a sweet wind carried her far, far away.